VOICES ON THE BRINK

VOICES ON THE BRINK
a border tale

Tom Marshall

Macmillan of Canada
A Division of Canada Publishing Corporation
Toronto, Ontario, Canada

CANADIAN CATALOGUING IN PUBLICATION DATA

Marshall, Tom, date.
  Voices on the brink

ISBN 0-7715-9913-7

I. Title.

PS8576.A758V64   1989   C813'.54   C88-095371-3
PR9199.3.M385V64   1989

Designed by David Montle

Printed in Canada

Macmillan of Canada
A Division of Canada Publishing Corporation
Toronto, Ontario, Canada

ACKNOWLEDGEMENTS

Two brief sections of this novel have appeared in *Quarry* (Spring, 1987).

I would like also to acknowledge here the good advice and assistance of Bella Pomer, my agent, and of Philippa Campsie, my editor. And to express my appreciation as well to those friends whose general moral support has helped me more than they know over the last few years to persist in writing my books in discouraging times as well as good ones.

"Perpetually the eye is on the verge of descrying a pattern in this weaving, and perpetually it is cheated by change. . . ."

— Rupert Brooke (1913)

In the eye is the wound.

Lancings of pity, blades of sensual disappointment
Have pierced the delicate pupil.
Transfixed, the bird of heavenly airs
Is struck at sundown,
Entering the leafy wood. . . .

— Douglas LePan, "The Wounded Prince" (1948)

Where am I? A tunnel, cold stone. Walls. Dark. Ahead somewhere there is a roaring. Light. Windsound. The damp. It is so damp here. Lisan. I am looking for Lisan. There is a roaring. . . . Voices. Many voices. I am naked as I lurch drunkenly toward them. Down, down. . . . Stone walls in darkness. My skin is touched, pricked now with wet blowdarts. I shiver uncontrollably as if on fire. . . . Fire. The city is in flames above us. White, utter white. My open eyes. Blind sight. Voices. The voice of power. Fire-storm. Planet dying. ". . . neither will we shrink from that risk. . . ." Skinpricks. A fiery wetness envelops me. Lisan, where are you? The roar is deafening, the white spray bursts from opening walls. World spume, waterfire. . . . White. I am falling, falling. . . .

Till I awake to dawnlight. Silence. Ordinary day. The nightmare done. Again. Sweating. Safe. Safe. The white institutional room cool around me.

PROLOGUE: The Cut

There are insane places on the earth, and at one of them I grew up.

Today, if you look along the short street from the corner where I lived between the ages of six and twenty-four to that interruption of natural order we called "the cut", there is (incongruously to me though not, of course, to the children who live on these streets now) a tourist's observation-tower rising in the near distance beyond the tops of the trees and houses on the other side. The tower stands on an unseen hill sloping steeply down to the even steeper cliffs of an invisible river in order to view from above a here-invisible — though often audible — pair of large waterfalls. Except for the tower, everything here in these hot streets is much as it was thirty years ago.

These tacky, rundown houses. An old song comes to mind: "Ontario's bound to be shabby genteel." It is July 1978. I am a ghost here on this sweltering afternoon that has emptied the streets of people. No one comes. I am invisible. I am a time-traveler from the past.

"The cut". It is that violation of the land that enabled an

extension of the Queen Elizabeth highway to slope more gently than it otherwise would have done down to the bridge that takes one to the United States. So that there are cliffs, small ones but steeper and higher part way down to the river, on each side of the highway. On my side the path on the top of the cliff is now overgrown with sumacs and tangles of other trees and bushes. Here we liked to play, never considering that it might be dangerous.

At the cut my friend Carl and I used to drop small stones just behind the moving people and cars below. "Crazy Carl" I called him. We never hit anyone, nor did we really mean to. We did bomb the tops of cars from the Palmer Street bridge, though. This was our war game. Carl and I. We called it "Hiroshima". Feeling powerful and safe up there. Till we were caught at it and lectured in a friendly rather than hostile fashion by Bennie Smith, an older boy.

At the cut I had one of my earliest near-disasters. Crawling under a loose barbed-wire fence near the upper end of the path into somebody's backyard I scratched my right eyelid. There wasn't much pain so at first I thought nothing of it. But then there was blood on my face. So I went home. I had scratched a hole in my eyelid. My mother was not amused. The doctor — Dr. Palmer, Carl's father — had to sew it together on the dining-room table, and I wore an eyepatch for weeks. But no permanent damage was done.

My eyes were open day and night. I was a frequent insomniac. On the walls and ceiling of the bedroom there was wallpaper with abstract patterns on it. I could still see it in the dark, vibrating, making pictures. The pictures were of animals, a wood, stories that I now realize came from within me, not from the wall. They were hallucinations, I suppose, projections from the unconscious. I thought nothing of it, I merely watched, fascinated. A psychic or Rorschach cinema. A little later, when I had read all the Greek and Norse mythology in the public library, I saw myself as the child Orpheus in the wood. I lived much of the time in another world. The "land of faery", I guess — I sometimes thought of myself as a changeling — or the unconscious.

Sometimes I lay along the end of the bed for hours and looked down through the small window to the street. The street-light, the sidewalk, the lawns, the trees. I saw the night world in vivid streaks, vibrations. Everything seemed to be writhing like a mass of snakes. I was at ease then, as I am not always now, on the night side of things, receiving. I could hear the waterfalls roaring, the clanking trains that went by down at the end of our street. Then the waterfalls again.

> Who, if I cried, would hear me among the angelic
> orders? And even if one of them suddenly
> pressed me against his heart, I should fade in the strength of his
> stronger existence. For Beauty's nothing
> but beginning of Terror we're still just able to bear. . . .

I did not know that then. That the waterfalls, the arched "Canadian" falls and the straighter "American" falls, were dangerous as well as beautiful. "Each single angel is terrible," writes Rilke. Each contains the "invisible". Even now the falls are insidiously attractive to the potential suicide. Listen.

> Half a mile or so above the Falls, on either side, the water of the great stream begins to run more swiftly and in confusion. It descends with ever-growing speed. It begins chattering and leaping, breaking into a thousand ripples,

throwing up joyful fingers of spray. Sometimes it is divided by islands and rocks, sometimes the eye can see nothing but a waste of laughing, springing, foamy waves, turning, crossing, even seeming to stand for an instant erect, but always borne impetuously forward like a crowd of triumphant feasters. Sit close down by it, and you see a fragment of the torrent against the sky, mottled, steely, and foaming, leaping onward in far-flung criss-cross strands of water. Perpetually the eye is on the verge of descrying a pattern in this weaving, and perpetually it is cheated by change. In one place part of the flood plunges over a ledge a few feet high and a quarter of a mile or so long, in a uniform and stable curve. It gives an impression of almost military concerted movement, grown suddenly out of confusion. But it is swiftly lost again in the multitudinous tossing merriment. Here and there a rock close to the surface is marked by a white wave that faces backwards and seems to be rushing madly upstream, but is really stationary in the headlong charge. But for these signs of reluctance, the waters seem to fling themselves on with some foreknowledge of their fate, in an ever wilder frenzy. But it is no Maeterlinckian prescience. They prove, rather, that Greek belief that the great crashes are preceded by a louder merriment and a wilder gaiety. Leaping in the sunlight, careless, entwining, clamorously joyful, the waves riot on towards the verge.

But there they change. As they turn to the sheer descent, the white and blue and slate-colours, in the heart of the Canadian Falls at least, blend and deepen to a rich, wonderful, luminous green. On the edge of disaster the river seems to gather herself, to pause, to lift a head noble in ruin, and then, with a slow grandeur, to plunge into the eternal thunder and white chaos below. Where the stream runs shallower it is a kind of violet colour, but both violet and green fray and frill to white as they fall. The mass of water, striking some ever-hidden base of rock, leaps up the whole two hundred feet again in pinnacles and domes of spray. The spray falls back into the lower river once more; all but a little that fines to foam and white mist, which drifts in layers along the air, graining it, and wanders out on the wind over the trees and gardens and houses, and so vanishes.

Thus Rupert Brooke in 1913: no doubt the coming "great crash" of war informed his poet's sight. But some things do not change very quickly. It is still the best description. Brooke noted also the omnipresence about the falls of "touts", people trying to sell you things. I wonder what he would make of the proliferation of wax museums today.

In somewhat earlier times another visiting poet, Oscar Wilde, paradoxically less "Victorian" and more "modern" and ironic than Brooke, had managed (as Brooke to his chagrin could not) to be dismissive about the falls themselves. He wrote: "When I first saw the falls I was disappointed in the outline. Every American bride is taken there, and the sight must be one of the earliest, if not the keenest, disappointments of American married life."

These are men passed into the invisible. From here, now, all I can see is the tower that did not exist at the time of my childhood and youth. Nor did I then care about the opinions of visiting British writers of the yet-uncreated recent past. I heard the roaring. I meandered along the train tracks at the bottom of the street. I ate the mint leaves that grew out of railway cinders. I roamed the field beyond the tracks.

Beside the schoolground was another field where sometimes the grass was allowed to grow very tall. We liked to go there at recess. On the other side of the field was the Shredded Wheat factory, from which in spring there came a rich aroma of grain. Sometimes I think I catch that smell now in downtown Toronto. From a brewery, I suppose. The Americans have long since closed down the factory. The school has been torn down too.

Steve and Carl and Larry and I used to play games in the field of long grass. Four small boys. Myself and the three others who would figure in my disturbed future. Steve was the steady one, Carl the joker. Larry? Well, he was devious even then. Sly. But he tried to be ingratiating or funny, as some insecure or secretly angry children do. His father had been killed in the war. Carl really was funny. He had reddish-blond hair and very blue eyes that were always laughing. Steve was neutral in coloring, big for his age, a natural leader, good at baseball. I don't know what I was like then — I had no sense of myself. I lived in my older brother's and then my schoolfriends' shadows.

Then there was the war. That was always there in the background too, even after it was over. Hitler lived on in our children's lore, our games and songs. A great monster and so, perversely, a great hero. Looking at the fire in the fireplace I imagined Hitler's bunker in flames. I was Hitler. Or, alternatively, I was Hitler's son who must kill him in order to win the war and rescue my mother from his clutches. My father had a thin moustache at this time.

> Hitler
> has only got one ball,
> Goering
> has two but they're quite small,
> Himmler
> is somewhat similar,
> but poor old Goebbels
> has no balls
> at all.

I suppose we got that somehow from the returned soldiers. Probably Carl learned it first. Such songs pass from child to child like wildfire.

I'm looking under
a two-legged wonder
that I've underlooked before. . . .

Then there were the comic books. Each Saturday I went
down to Palmer Avenue, the street alongside the railroad
tracks, and walked across the bridge over the cut and the
highway and on for another block to the drugstore on the
corner of Victoria and Palmer. My weekly allowance was a
dime, so I bought one comic book a week. Captain Marvel
was my favorite. More than Superman. Captain Marvel
got his powers from Greek gods. I read at the age of ten
both comic books and Greek and Norse mythology. They
were both, after all, adventure stories. And the classic comics. I remember a version of Cyrano de Bergerac, who
disliked his own physical appearance just as much as I
disliked mine.

Superman was on the radio too in the years after the
war. Each afternoon before five o'clock I hurried home
away from Steve and Carl and the others, who went on
playing football or hockey. I was addicted to this radio
show. Instead of the usual commercials it had brief homilies against racial prejudice. While I ate a peanut-butter
sandwich I got the word from liberal America where
Superman and Batman lived. I much preferred the radio
version of Superman. Superman who was really mild-
mannered Clark Kent. Able to leap tall buildings at a single
bound. He had come as an infant from a dying planet in a
spaceship. My ballpoint pens at school were spaceships. So
were my overshoes plowing through the snow on my way
home from school.

I listened also, of course, in those years to Amos 'n'
Andy, and never thought then to connect them with the
Superman homilies. And on Sunday nights, Jack Benny
and his gang. Including Rochester, another comic black, a

servant. Followed by Benny's bandleader, Phil Harris, and Phil's wife, Alice Faye. My father said that she had previously been a movie star and singer, but on the radio she was only the somewhat shrewish wife of a bibulous husband. Their quarrels were horrendous. Followed by Edgar Bergen and Charlie McCarthy and Mortimer Snerd. (I saw them in a Walt Disney movie once too.) Followed by Fred Allen, whose jokes puzzled me.

At some point I was given the record album of *Oklahoma!* and loved its innocent American exuberance.

I had been born here, in Canada. But in 1940, when I was two, the war took me away to the southern United States. My father was a research chemist who worked during the war for the Canadian government, who then loaned him to the British government, who quietly assisted the Americans. It was part of Roosevelt's covert war effort before the Americans were legally in the war.

On November 1, 1940, we arrived in Joplin, Missouri. 1610 Kentucky Avenue. Until June 1941. Then Redings' Mill, out Daniel Boone Road, a cottage with wood-stove and coal-oil lamps: 1941-42. Then Royal Heights in Joplin: September 1942 to May 1943. May and June: a motel in Memphis, Tennessee. Then the house in Memphis, the only place down there I can actually remember, with the fig tree that was barren — perhaps cursed by some irascible deity — in the backyard: from June to December of 1943.

There was gas rationing then, which made an automobile impractical and shopping difficult for my parents. Most of the people about were not helpful to strangers.

There was a man next door who was paralysed from the waist down. He was cared for by a manservant. He had been shot by a burglar who entered his house. His wife had then divorced him.

Behind the houses was a lane where the black people walked. They never walked on the streets. Strange dark people. Sometimes a black man singing. Jimmy, the boy from across the street, called them bogeymen and said that they would get you if you went out at night. But I don't recall ever being frightened of them. My brother and I got really scared only once when an older boy threatened us with a cap-pistol. We thought that it was a real gun and that he was really going to shoot us. The neighbors, with one or two exceptions, were generally unfriendly to "Yankees". The neighbor kids once threw rocks at us. My older brother got beaten up.

In Memphis I went to school for a while at the age of five. My older brother and Jimmy and I. There is a photograph of the three of us on the school steps. Three small white boys in white cotton shirts and white shorts.

At some point in all these travels, perhaps Memphis, I had an experience that I have always remembered. I was in a bathtub with a toy duck. I was, I guess, lulled into a condition of reverie by the water, the stillness of everything. But I had the most intense sense not just of déjà vu but that this moment, this time and place, had always been happening and always would be happening. Though I had no words for the experience then. (In a way the falls is the same: there is a great stillness in its endless movement. . . .)

Near the end of 1943 my father went back ahead of us to Canada. My father's mother came down from Toronto to help. But she took ill. She had a heart condition. So my mother had the task of getting us all, children and ailing mother, back to Canada.

We are on a train full of soldiers in uniform. It is noisy and boisterous. They are passing around hip flasks. My grandmother has been trying in vain to teach me how to tie my shoelaces. But now I am running about the aisles with my brother bothering the soldiers. Our mother is too exhausted to try to keep us still and quiet any more. This scene is perhaps more imagined than remembered.

In Toronto it was winter, ice and snow. We lived in my grandmother's house on a small crescent near Davenport Road till the spring. The latest of our way-stations, a three-story house, too narrow to be called large though it seemed large to me then, facing east. So that I saw the sun break through cold winter clouds from my late grandfather's front study. A glory of horses and chariots tumbling. Later there was a real horse, the milk-horse, who would trot a little way down the street if we said "Giddyup" to him. His breath and ours visible on the winter air.

Farther along Davenport there was a real castle, Casa Loma.

At school in Toronto we stood in a ring with our eyes closed and said morning prayers. The bolder children tiptoed toward the teacher in the center while we squinted and peered at them.

One day we got lost coming home from school. We were on the cold street crying. At last belonging nowhere. But someone, an older girl, I think, brought us back again to the right street.

Then we were moving again. Riding in a car with hills in the near distance. Hills on one side and a huge lake on the other.

Then here. To this old lilac tree in the front yard. This old brick house. (Long ago sold to Dutch immigrants. And they themselves long gone.) Another crescent street curving down to the railway tracks. A roaring in the air on spring nights. The trains clanking by. The small city on the river between the great lakes. The waterfalls.

To my father, a scientist, it didn't seem to matter too much where he was, where we went — in Canada or in the

States. One of his brothers became an American to get ahead in life. To my mother it mattered, though, for she came from an old Ontario family that had settled as Loyalists in Scarborough before 1800. But circumstances took her where they did, and brought me as well to live in this toxic border town. My father now worked again for an American chemical company.

In 1945 my father told me that the atom had been discovered not by the Americans or by the Germans but by the ancient Greeks. When they dropped the bombs on Hiroshima and Nagasaki to end the war that had so much directed our lives, I was here. . . .

ONE

◆

Growing up
in the shadow of the U.S.A. . . . .
— Dan Hill

"All I want," said Steve, "is to get my cock sucked in elegant surroundings."

"How about the cemetery?" said Carl.

"By Old Queen Harold," giggled Ron.

Steve did not deign to respond.

"Do you think her tits are really that big?"

They were cruising on their bicycles down the highway through the cut. It was a bright, cloudless day.

"No, jughead, they stuff her dresses."

"I think they're real," said Steve. Steve was the acknowledged authority on sex. He claimed that he had felt up Myra Stone in between their fathers' garages.

"Maybe I'll give her a hand-job and find out what's real," said Carl.

There was already a little crowd across the street from the General Brock Hotel. And near the entrance to the bridge in a roped-off area there were several cameras and cameramen and another man who must be the director.

Then into view from behind the cameras and cameramen she came. She was doing her special walk. Her wiggle.

"Oh, Marilyn," said Ron. The cameras pointed at her butt as she flicked it back and forth walking toward the carillon. She wore a tight red jacket and a tight skirt. The boys now watched in silence. Then someone in the crowd, a little drunk perhaps, Ron thought, shouted, "Shake it, baby!"

Everyone laughed. Except the director and the camera crew.

The director was annoyed. He halted the shooting abruptly.

"Can't you people," he said in loud exasperation to the small crowd, "be a little more courteous if you want to watch? It costs us time and money to keep doing this over and over." And more in this vein for several minutes. He had a broad American accent. Except for that, he seemed like one of their teachers reprimanding the class. There was nothing glamorous or exotic about him.

Then they shot the walk once more, the crowd keeping scrupulously quiet. And again. The boys watching avidly.

Until the star, with just one cameraman for escort, crossed the street hurriedly to the hotel. Ron rode his bicycle right up beside her to stare at her. She looked straight ahead, she had no expression. Or maybe she was a bit frightened. He took in her shiny blonde hair, her low-cut blouse, her tight dress. He was sure her tits were real. She wasn't wearing a brassiere, he was sure.

Then she was gone into the hotel. It was over almost before it had begun. A glimpse of the goddess.

"For God's sake," said Ron, "she's not even wearing a brassiere."

"She gets killed," said Carl. "In the carillon. By Joseph Cotten. He strangles her."

"I'd like to get *my* hands on her," said Steve.

A blonde in a tight dress. So close he might have touched her. Handled her.

"How do you feel?" said Ron automatically.

Steve and Carl in chorus: "*With my hands.*"

Ron said then, "I wonder how *she* feels about it, though?" About being strangled, extinguished. . . .

He had an image, quite unbidden, of a small girl, weeping inconsolably. . . .

Several years later Steve and Carl bought an old Chevy. Each Friday the guys went over the river to drink beer and sometimes eat pizza. "Hangers and hops" Carl called this meal. The drinking age was twenty-one in Ontario and eighteen in New York State, but in the latter case nobody tried very hard to enforce it — the Canadian kids brought over too much business. Steve and Carl and Ron had been going over since they were sixteen.

First they would cruise along through the crowd down by the Canadian falls looking for pretty American women. The colored lights on the falls would be turned on. American women were supposed to be "faster" than Canadian women. Even the new brides: they had heard some remarkable stories about new brides and "gang bangs" even if they hadn't yet had the good fortune to check them out. American women were all "sex-crazy" — it said so in the paperback skin-books in the drugstore at Victoria and Palmer. After the falls and the park it was over the bridge and into the other more active city. Looking out on the crowded streets from the back seat of the car, Ron sometimes had a wild longing to know everyone, every face, in the moving crowd. He felt their loneliness and wildness, that American restlessness, he felt as if he was catching it, catching them like a disease.

Steve had a steady girlfriend whom he saw Saturday nights. But he liked to look around.

Carl and Ron were virgins until each went, on separate occasions, into the field of long grass between the public school and the Shredded Wheat factory with Jane Berners, a plump red-headed girl who would cheerfully fuck with just about anybody. She was a "hoo-er" who didn't charge. It was even said that she and her girlfriend Rita French were also lesbians. Carl was so nervous the first time he went with her that she gave him a bit of a blow-job to get him going. After he had laid her he shoved grass in her cunt and ran away laughing while she yelled at him. After that he went back to her fairly frequently, not telling his buddies. But Ron, a romantic, wanted something less squalid than humping with your pants down around your legs in a field.

Sometimes they went to strip joints over the river. Mostly the strippers seemed middle-aged to them and physically slightly gross. Once they saw a comic kneel down before a buxom lady's barely covered crotch. She was otherwise naked, having finished her routine. Her large melony breasts were pendulous. "Whaddya think yer doing?" she demanded. "Kissing Castro," he replied. Such snappy repartee was standard in these places.

Saturday they went their separate ways. Sometimes Ron or Carl had a date with a "nice" girl. Or sometimes they might go to a movie over the river or in Buffalo together. On Sundays in the summer five or six of the guys would go to the beach to look at the girls there. It was a restless time.

If only there was something, or someone, I really wanted, Ron thought. He was good in school, without caring very much. He assumed he would go to university afterwards. Maybe that would open up something. Meanwhile there was only this lethargy. This waiting for something to happen.

He was lying on his back on the bed thinking gloomy thoughts. It was a Friday afternoon in October. He had come straight home from the collegiate, which was only half a block away. He was even more bored than usual.

His bedroom was now at the back corner of the house between the bathroom and a stairway that went down to the kitchen. His older brother, who had finished high school and was working at the chemical company over the river, still had the bedroom that they had once shared at the front of the house. He remembered idly how he had often been an insomniac as a child, how he had looked down from the end of the top of the bunk bed through the corner window to the street. Now he had a window on the narrower street that led from the cut to the circle within which was the collegiate.

His parents, his brother, none of them understood his restlessness, he felt. He couldn't account for it himself. Why wasn't he solid and practical like Mike? Mike would marry his girlfriend Lois as soon as he could afford to, and leave home.

He didn't even like to read as much as he used to. Too much school. University had better be more interesting than this, he thought. Thank God it was Friday. At the age of thirteen he had thought maybe he would like to be a writer. Now he was indifferent to everything. The guys were going to Buffalo tonight. Anything to get out of the rut.

Steve and Carl would be over at Victoria Avenue now at Ernie's Lunch. He had wanted to be alone. "We'll pick you up later," Steve said. Steve was always the initiator, he had the car. He was the one who said, "Let's go to Buffalo," or "Let's go see some strippers," or whatever. Though tonight's peculiar excursion was Carl's idea.

In Ron's head Carl sang a song he had made up:

> I wish I had a mustache,
> I wish I had a beard,
> 'cause if I had a mustache
> and if I had a beard
> then I would be feared. . . .

"Hey, ya know what a 'willnot' is? A little piece of shit that gets caught in your asshair and simply *will not* come out."

"As for Benson here, he takes it in the left ear. . . ."

I'd like to go very far away, Ron thought. Like half-way around the world. At dinner his mother would say, as she always did on Fridays, "Where are you going tonight, Ron?" and he would mumble, "I don't know, we haven't decided." Why not say instead, "To Morocco. Greece. Acapulco. And I'm not coming back."

He lacked the energy to go anywhere, he knew. And where would he get the money? He had to go to university and get a job. Though no job he had ever heard of appealed to him.

Carl was planning to go to California next year and go to school there. California.

He could hear his brother in the bathroom next door. He was home from work then and would be hungry. Ron hoped that he wouldn't come in. All he ever said to him any more was that he should know what it was like to work nine to five. Later he would take his girlfriend to the movies or something. Ron wondered how much Mike was getting from Lois. It had been two years since they had started going together. She wore his fraternity pin on her sweater over one of her impressive boobs. She was a nice enough girl, if no great beauty or anything.

He heard Mike go away again.

Soon he would have to slip down the back stairs and join them for supper. Or else somebody would yell up at him.

He went into the bathroom and washed his hands. In the mirror he saw a full head of black hair over a slightly sullen and yet strangely innocent face. He had hollow cheeks, large dark eyes, a straight nose, thin lips, and a markedly cleft chin. Not movie-star handsome, he had long ago decided, but not ugly either. His expression was usually a studied blankness.

"Ron-nie," called his mother up the back stairs.

"I'm coming."

He combed his hair a little more. He disliked his own looks but decided that they would have to do.

He clattered down the steep back stairs to the kitchen and then went into the dining-room.

Ron's father rarely spoke to his sons at the supper table or on any other occasion. He had grown more and more silent with the years. Ron seemed to remember that he had been more talkative, more informative and forthcoming, when they were small. About the war, the world in general. When had he fallen silent?

Ron's mother — he sometimes thought — never stopped talking. She was a nervous little woman who could not bear a silence. Her husband's silences were not companionable silences.

"I saw Iris today at the supermarket. She looked old. Old."

"Iris who?" asked Mike. Apparently just to say something. His father, a brooding, heavy man, seemed perfectly indifferent to Iris.

"Iris Weathers. She went to school with your father. Was supposed to be the prettiest girl in the school."

"Well, time passes," said Mr. Benson.

"*Sick* transit," said Ron.

"Don't be smart," said his mother.

"That's Latin," said Mike. "Already I can't remember any of the stuff."

"Are you seeing Lois tonight?" she asked.

"Yeah."

"Ron, where are you going?"

"We haven't decided."

After supper he went up and combed his hair again.

At seven o'clock Steve's horn was honking outside his bedroom window. So he went down and out to them. He wore a jacket over a blue V-neck sweater and gray pants. It was cool and dark outside.

He got into the back seat. Barry, a new friend of Steve's, was there. Carl and Steve were in the front seat. It was their car.

"Hear about the girl who loved Italians?" said Carl. "She never let a dago by without getting laid."

"I could pass for an Italian," said Ron.

"But you're not one."

"Let's cruise Centre Street," said Steve. "Run down a couple of the bruisers."

The corner of Centre Street and Victoria Avenue was where the Centre Street gang hung out. You could drive by to look at them but you couldn't stop or walk around there if you didn't want to get beaten up. It was their territory.

"Naw, let's head straight for Buffalo," said Carl.

"Yeah," said Ron.

They had decided to visit a queer bar in Buffalo to see what queers really looked like. Someone had told Steve that Harold Fanstone, "Old Queen Harold," went there. Harold worked in a bank downtown. It was said that he drove guys into the cemetery grounds and sucked them off there. Carl claimed that Harold had once propositioned him. Carl, Steve, and Ron had in the past had discussions about whether they would let a guy blow them. Steve said it was disgusting to contemplate. Carl said that in a certain mood you wouldn't care. But as long as there were girls in the world you didn't need a queer. There was always Jane Berners.

It was a forty-five-minute drive to Fort Erie and then over the Peace Bridge to Buffalo. Ron felt as always the exhilaration of moving fast over the highway in the darkness. If only they could keep going, never come back. It didn't matter where.

Over the bridge, into the huge city of shadows. Kingdom of night. Once, last year, on a Buffalo street, looking idly out of the car window, wishing that he could *be* every one of the restless crowd of bodies, faces, Ron had seen a man in the crowd stick a knife suddenly into another man's stomach. The car had gone on, the others hadn't seen it. He didn't even tell them. I might be the only one, he thought, in all this mass of people who saw it. It happened so fast.

Now they were cruising along a street of bars and hotels, looking at the black prostitutes. When they had parked and were sitting in the car one came over. Carl rolled down the window.

The girl leaned in, and looked them over boldly.

"You boys lookin' for some fun? I know a place where there's everythin' you like. All kinds of girls. Even some boys for boys who like boys. Now, you" — she pointed at

Barry, who was thin and intense-looking — "you look like the kind of guy who likes boys. Right? We got some nice young boys."

All the others laughed. Barry attempted to take it in stride.

"I like the look of *you*," he said aggressively.

"Come on, then. It's just 'round the corner."

"Maybe we should all go," said Carl.

Ron thought it might be dangerous to go into some strange house full of Negroes, that the girl might even be diseased.

"How much?" said Barry.

"Ten bucks. More, if you want extra kicks."

"I want my cock sucked."

"That's extra."

"Aw, fuck off," said Barry. He didn't really want to go with her, Ron saw.

"I knew you was queer," she said, drifting away. She had black frizzy hair, chocolate skin, a black coat on. She was probably in her twenties, not bad-looking. "You punks are a waste of time."

"Fuck off," yelled Steve after her.

"Let's get off the Negro streets," said Carl. "Or we'll get our tires slashed."

They drove on to another street of bars.

"There it is," said Carl. The Wild Side. Said to be a queer bar. They parked the car once again, and got out, locking the doors.

There was a policeman on duty outside the bar. But he paid them no attention as they went in.

There was a juke-box playing Bill Haley and the Comets. A bar, tables, a lot of guys sitting around. It looked quite ordinary. Except that there were no women. They sat down at a table.

It was a bit disappointing. "Let's just have a beer and see if anything interesting happens," said Carl.

They ordered draft beer.

After a while the place got a bit more lively. Guys drifted from table to table greeting friends. Some of their faces when they talked took on a slightly feverish animation. Others sullenly eyed whoever came in the door. Occasionally men embraced, confirming Carl's information about the place and shocking Steve. Anybody who went by on the street could see in through the large front window.

"Do you see old Harold around?" asked Ron.

"No. But I think I recognize that guy over there," said Carl.

Ron looked. It was a thin, short guy of about their own age. Yes. It was Larry Brown. He had been a prize-winning boy soprano in public school. Later he disappeared from town and it was said that he had become the boyfriend of someone in the Mafia in Buffalo. One of those crazy rumors.

"I hope he doesn't recognize us," said Steve.

But he had. He came over, swinging his hips in a slightly exaggerated Marilyn Monroe fashion. He had always been rather effeminate, Ron remembered, everyone had always assumed he was "that way." But he was amusing, nobody really disliked him. They had only teased him a lot, thought Ron now.

"*Well*," Larry said. "All the boys from Hicksville where I went to school. Checking out how the other half lives?" And he sat down at their table.

"You might say," said Carl. "How are you, Larry? You live in Buffalo now?"

"Oh *yes*. For years and years. I've got a special friend here. But what brings you, my old innocent playmates, to sin city?"

"As you said, curiosity," said Ron. Oddly enough, they were not uneasy or embarrassed at all, except for Steve.

"Is it always this quiet in this place?" asked Barry.

"It is," said Larry, "Until the after-hours club opens upstairs and there's dancing."

"Dancing. You mean guys actually dance with each other?" said Carl.

"Don't knock it till you've tried it," said Larry.

"We're just having a look," Steve assured him.

"I'll keep your secret," said Larry. "Some of the boys here might not take too kindly to the idea of being laughed at. I mean the tougher, more butch types that are into leather and motorcycles. You ought to meet some of them."

A queer Centre gang? Denizens of the night world where all was strange? For some reason, though it was Friday, Ron remembered now the rhyme about "Thursday the day the fairies play". Larry was a little drunk, he thought. He needed to chatter on at them, it seemed.

"I'm a stranger here myself now," he went on. "I'm not allowed to come here any more. But my friend is out of town, so I thought I'd just look in on the old place. If he knew I was here I could end up in the lake in cement." He giggled over this thought.

"Let's go," said Steve, "where there are women." He had become uneasy.

"Yeah, let's blow this cave," said Ron.

"What?" said Carl, delighted. "*Blow?*"

"I know a place," said Larry quickly. "Near here. Let me take you there."

"As long as there are girls," laughed Carl. "We've done this scene, and that's probably enough of queer life for one lifetime. It's pretty uninteresting."

"Most of us are harmless," said Larry. "Even boring. My trouble is that I've always liked the violent types."

They went out in a body and then along the street to the other bar. Ron reflected for what seemed to be the hundredth time that Buffalo was a physically dirty city, designed for corruption.

The new bar had an easier atmosphere. There was not the slight but noticeable tension that there had been in The Wild Side.

There was a girl, not more than twenty, Ron thought, sitting at the bar talking to the waiter. She had black hair and was very pretty. Larry seemed to know her, for he left them at a table and went over to talk to her.

"Felicia, dear," Ron heard him greet her.

Felicia.

She was talking with Larry. Then she turned to look at their table. Larry was explaining them, it seemed. God, she was quite beautiful. What did a girl like that have to do with a pathetic creature like Larry?

Larry came back to the table.

"Who is *that?*" said Carl.

"My friend Felicia. Actually, she's my friend's sister. I told her you were wild Canadian boys looking for American girls. Since you have no taste, I had to rescue you from possible trouble in The Wild Side."

"Why don't you ask her to join us?" said Carl.

"She thinks you must be queer if you're with me," giggled Larry. "Though I told her Steve was straight to the point of paralysis."

"Straight?" repeated Carl. The term was unfamiliar.

Ron could not take his eyes away from Felicia.

Sensing this, she came over.

"Do sit down, Felicia," said Larry. "These boys are all in love with you already."

She sat down. Everybody was introduced. She asked them about Canada. She was soft-spoken, almost ladylike. Even Carl behaved himself in her presence. She wore a simple skirt and sweater. She was young but she seemed experienced, knowing.

"Do you come here often?" said Ron.

"My brother doesn't like me coming here," she said. "But he's out of town."

The mysterious brother seemed to dislike bars. Was he really in the Mafia? Nobody had dared to ask Larry.

"Are you Italian?" asked Ron.

"Partly."

"Where do you live?"

"Near here."

"Do you go to school?"

"I quit."

After a while she said to Larry: "Walk me home."

"Oh, Felicia, *just* when I'm enjoying myself with old schoolmates."

"I will," said Ron without thought.

"All right," she said. She got up and put on her coat.

Steve and Carl were surprised. They had rarely seen Ron take the initiative like this.

Felicia and Ron went out into the street. At the first corner they turned onto a dark street with large houses.

"Do you live with your brother?"

"No," she laughed. "He lives with Larry."

"Do you mind that?"

"It's what he wants." Her tone was matter-of-fact. "I have my own apartment downtown here. My parents wouldn't pay for it but my brother pays the rent. Since I quit the convent school."

"How old are you?"

"None of your business. I'm eighteen. And *old* for eighteen."

"I'm going to university next year," said Ron.

"I didn't want that."

He looked at her. But her face was in shadow.

"What do you want?"

"Not that." Then: "I want to be free."

"Yes," he said. "But what does that mean?"

"We're here," she said. "I won't ask you up."

"Can I see you again?"

"Maybe. Maybe I'll be at the bar again tomorrow night." And she began to walk along the driveway of a house toward the side door.

"All right," he called after her. "I'll look for you tomorrow."

Why did I say that, he thought as he walked quickly back. I haven't the slightest idea what she's like.

He found the guys in the parked car.

"We almost left you to your fate," said Carl. "We had to get away from poor old Larry. He was getting kind of weepy. About the old days at Kitchener Street Public School, for Christ's sake."

Ron got in.

"Well, that was a quick lay," said Steve.

"Don't be crude," said Ron.

"No comment, eh?" And they all laughed.

Ron said: "I expect you guys all got quick blow-jobs from old weepy Larry."

Steve turned the key in the ignition. Then they were moving again in the night that was now charged with excitement. I'll come back, thought Ron, and find her. In this dark city. She had no last name. He hadn't even bothered to look at the street sign. But he could find it from the bar.

Steve turned on the car radio. A group of husky voices were singing a song called "Earth Angel".

He woke up early with a new sense of urgency. Of longing. He had been dreaming strange and vivid dreams again. Of black men with knives. . . . Of the whole city in flames: so that he wondered if this meant that they had dropped the bomb. . . . Then, in a small room at the city's dark heart he was with the girl, Felicia. . . . He was touching her delicately beautiful face as the city burned and collapsed all around them. . . .

But morning is a different, less compelling country. Not like the magic kingdom of the night. It is a bright ordinary day, the light has wakened him. He is alone again. As always.

Wild and sweet. . . . Nights that were wild and sweet, wild and sweet. Excitement on the air. Only it was always someone else who found it, grasped it.

Why did he think that she was the one?

I have to borrow a car. Either Mike's car or Steve's or Carl's car. Steve and Carl alternated on Saturdays. Today was Carl's day. Too bad. He would demand more details, even before considering it. Steve would have been less curious. But Mike was out, he wouldn't let his car go to Buffalo.

He found Carl in his backyard. He was cleaning it up for his old man. His old man was their family doctor.

Ron helped him silently for a while.

Then Carl said: "You want something from me, or something?"

"How can you tell?"

"You're being so goddam helpful, for a change."

They both laughed.

"I suppose," said Carl, "it's the 'family' car."

"Yeah, well, it's like this. I've got a date with that girl. I need some wheels. Just for tonight."

"Ohhh. You're moving fast, are you?"

"I just have a feeling that if I don't turn up tonight I won't see her again. She'll disappear or something."

He did not know why he said that, the words just came out.

"She's a good-looking broad," said Carl. "But I didn't think she was all *that* special."

"Look. Have you got a date tonight?"

"Yeah."

"So you want the car?"

"Well, I did pay for it. Look. Here's what I'll do, if you're so sold on this dago broad. I'll take Betty to the movies in Buffalo. We'll drop you at that bar. And meet you there again at twelve o'clock."

"All right. I'd appreciate it." Though now he wouldn't be able to drive her anywhere. But he didn't think he'd ask Carl for the car while they were in the movie. Getting there was enough.

"I've got to get Betty home by one. So you'll have to make like Cinderella and meet us at twelve."

"All right." he felt a huge relief.

Good old Carl. You could rely on him in an emergency. Always clowning around. He remembered then for no very obvious reason the time when they were kids and they had taken some huge truck tires from the big garage near Carl's house and rolled them down the street into the traffic on Victoria Avenue. The garagemen had sworn and yelled at them. As kids they were always sneaking into that garage. It was their favorite forbidden territory.

Carl and Ron had been friends even before they went to school. Carl was the instigator of all their wilder pranks. He was an only child, indulged by his parents in most things. At public school he always had money for candy which he would share with Ron and Steve. And even with Larry, who used, Ron now remembered, to hang around Steve as much as he could get away with. He was barely tolerated by the others at that time, and often made the butt of Carl's crueler jokes.

Larry. Who would have thought? Larry the fairy. In Grade One they had pulled down his pants in front of the girls. Later he won a small cup for singing a treble solo in a city-wide competition. Then he was made to do his prize-winning piece again for the school assembly. Carl and Ron and Steve had laughed at him, and for months afterward mocked the pseudo-English vowel tones of his flute-like rendition of "Cherry Ripe". Who would have thought that he would now lead Ron to a beautiful girl in Buffalo?

I am in love, thought Ron lightly, with an American girl. American. . . . Mr. Groat, their Grade Six teacher, had hated Americans, he now remembered. He told the class that the Americans were selfish cowards who had stayed out of both world wars until the last minute, and then taken all the glory afterwards. They were bullies. "A bully is always a coward underneath," he instructed. Mr. Groat also hated French Canadians. For he had not managed to make it overseas in the Second World War himself. He had been stationed instead in the Gaspé peninsula, where he had been mortally offended by the "pea-soupers" because of their refusal to stand up for the singing of The King at the movies. But he also hated Edward VIII, now Duke of Windsor, for letting the monarchy down. "He was always a bum. He was never fit to be king." Perhaps Mr. Groat hated most people, even himself. He was a petty sadist who had punished minor or imaginary misbehavior or inattentiveness on whim with the dreaded leather strap. Behind his back they had called him "Hitler".

Carl dropped Ron off at the second bar of the previous night. It was called the Flamingo, he now noticed.

Felicia was not there. But it was early.

What if she didn't come?

He didn't want to drink. He decided to walk over to the house she lived in, hoping he could distinguish it from the others. Or even find the right street.

He turned on to the street he thought that they had taken the previous night. The houses were much alike: old brick, narrow, too close together, without very much in the way of front lawns. But he thought that it was about the fourth house.

He went along the driveway to the side door.

There was no nameplate, only a buzzer. He pushed it. What the hell, he thought, if it's the wrong house, it's the wrong house.

Someone came down the stairs on the other side of the door. A female shape in the darkness.

She opened the door.

"Oh. It's you. I was afraid it must be my brother. Or I wouldn't have answered."

What does that mean, he thought.

"Larry's here. He's hiding from my brother," Felicia said in her matter-of-fact way.

"I wanted to see you again," he said awkwardly.

"You'd better come in. Maybe you can help. You're an old friend of his, aren't you?"

Hardly, he thought, as he followed her up the stairs.

The main room of the apartment was simple. A sofa, some old chairs, a plant. Larry sat on the sofa. He had a black eye and looked as if he might have been crying.

"He came back unexpectedly?" Ron asked.

"Last night. He found Larry high on speed. And not alone."

Ron felt out of his depth. He didn't know what "speed" was. Some drug, obviously. He had a horror of drugs and "dope fiends". He felt maybe he had made a mistake in coming back to Buffalo. Also, Felicia didn't seem so extraordinarily beautiful tonight. Something about her chilled him. She was so young and yet so cool about it all.

"He'll kill me," said Larry. He looked a bit calmer now, as if the thought steadied him.

"Has this happened before?" asked Ron.

"Once," Larry said.

"At least," said Felicia coldly.

"I used to sing in the bars," said Larry. "I loved it. But after I met Angelo he wouldn't let me sing any more." He sounded like a petulant child.

Then the phone rang. Ron started at the shrill sound, but Larry and Felicia seemed to have expected it. Felicia let it ring several times before answering it.

"I'll talk to him," said Larry. He seemed to have pulled

himself together in just a few minutes, Ron thought.

"Yes. All right," said Felicia tonelessly to the telephone. Larry took it from her.

"This is the only place he's safe from him," said Felicia to Ron.

"All right," said Larry equally calmly. He put down the receiver.

"I'm going home," he said. "Thanks."

"Phone," she said, "if things get rough."

"I will."

Larry went down the stairs and let himself out. He said nothing to Ron. He seemed in a bit of a daze.

Felicia looked at Ron.

"This whole episode will excite my brother," she said. "I know him."

Ron felt a bit sick.

"Larry likes being slapped around a bit, too. What a pair."

"You're very cool about it all," said Ron.

"I'm used to them."

"I guess."

"I can't go out. He might phone. Do you want a drink?"

"Yeah," said Ron.

"I could use the company for a while," she said.

To be alone with her at her place. But this was not quite how he had imagined it, dreamed it. . . .

She made him a Scotch on the rocks. "This is what my dear brother likes," she said sarcastically. She was wearing a simple skirt, a different sweater from the one of the evening before. It seemed a long time ago now. She was darkly lovely, he decided again. She looked older than eighteen.

"Don't you see your parents?" he asked.

"I suppose you still live with yours," she replied scornfully. She was on edge, harder than she had been the night before. It occurred to him then that probably she was frightened.

She seemed to read his thought.

"My brother," she said, "is calmer when I'm around. You might say I'm a moderating influence."

"It must have been difficult," he offered.

"At times. But I can handle it. I've seen a lot, I can tell you. Do you think you still want to know me better?"

"Yes. I do."

She smiled then, though somewhat ruefully.

The Scotch was relaxing him a little. He wondered what they might say or do next. He was sitting on the sofa where Larry had been while she sat primly on a chair.

"My brother is a lot older than I am. He was a teenager when I was a child. When he left home I was the only thing in the family that he cared about. And he had reason to feel responsible for me."

"He's got another family now," suggested Ron.

"No comment," she said.

"I want to know you better."

She got up and came over to sit beside him. Then she took hold of the left side of his face with her right hand and kissed him firmly and efficiently.

"I've never kissed a Canadian before,' she said. "An innocent Canadian."

"We're not so innocent," Ron said.

Then the phone. Felicia went pale. She picked it up immediately.

"Yes?"

There was an audible click at the other end of the line.

"That's a signal, I know it is. We'll have to go over there. Have you got a car?"

"No. And I'm not going. It's none of my business."

"We'll get a taxi. Please come, I need someone with me."

She dialed a number hastily.

In the taxi she kept saying, "Why was it so quiet? I couldn't hear either of their voices."

They got out at an expensive-looking apartment building.

They were well away from the rundown area of town. Ron found himself paying the surly black driver.

"There are lights on in the apartment," said Felicia. They went in. She was a bit frantic now, no longer pretending to be cool. They took the elevator to the sixth floor.

The door of the apartment was slightly ajar, as if they were expected. But there was no sound from within.

A large, elegant room with modern Danish furniture and real paintings on the walls, not at all like Felicia's rather shabby but comfortable living-room.

"Angelo? Where are you? Where's Larry?"

Felicia went along a hall toward an open door where there was a light on. She didn't come back.

He did not at first follow. Surely it was none of his business; he had merely escorted Felicia through the dark city.

So he allowed a few minutes to pass. But there was no sound at all from the other room; it was as if first Angelo and Larry and now Felicia too had been swallowed up by nothingness and silence.

He found himself moving carefully along the dark hall

toward the lighted doorway. The center of the maze, he thought, for no obvious reason. Of the wicked and glamorous night city. . . .

"Felicia?" He sounded strange to himself. The name was strange. What was going on?

She was sitting in a chair staring at a piece of paper. A note. He could hear her breathing now. It was the bedroom. On the large double bed lying on his back was a naked man, a powerful male body. Ron stared at him. The man's eyes were open, questioning; it was not an especially cruel face. He was slightly overweight but powerfully muscular. His throat had been cut. There was a lot of blood. He was going bald, Ron saw, but his body from his neck and his large shoulders down to his ankles was the hairiest he had ever seen. His curled penis looked unnaturally small for such a powerful ape's body.

Then Felicia began to scream.

TWO

◆

That city is a time-warp.

"This play is memory," says Tom Wingfield in *The Glass Menagerie*, a work I admire. Tom is, of course, a version of Tom ("Tennessee") Williams.

I too am composing a fiction. Of sorts. I too am making in my head the "play" or the "novel" of my young life. It takes place mainly in the city I have here presented, an imaginary city. That is, the city as I remember it is both real *and* imaginary. The city is a time-warp. I don't mean Buffalo, of course, but rather my native city.

Once this was, for Europeans, the symbol of America: a savage force, a beginning or a last end. I mean that mental image of the waterfall. The endless majestic descent, to silent mental thunder: that green-and-white torrent of birth and death, ideal symbol of the new land. Glamorous, challenging, dangerous, a vast unexplored wilderness of energy.

"By 1900, though," a journalist writes, "the falls had been eclipsed by other icons, especially the Statue of Liberty, as *the* symbol of America. Besides, Canada had the better falls."

For there are, after all, two falls.

All nineteenth-century descriptions of the place remark upon the incongruity of such grandeur, such a fountain of eternal energy, terror, and delight, encroached upon by the tawdry tourist commerce and utterly tasteless gimmickry. Here, they say, is natural poetry exploited and debased by philistine western man. Here is a pristine, impossibly pure, nobly savage Canada at America's raw edge.

"Only man is vile." But these days the river itself is a conduit of rank chemical corruption from country to country.

The play is memory. I have re-invented it, set words down. I, Ronald Benson, middle-aged, not always sane. In this swift process, this flow, pure inventions will partly erase whatever might really have happened — as a new, intermittent laying down of tracks will partly erase an old, original, true tune, or pentimento "improve" upon a pictured first world. Yet something persists in this inevitable layering/erosion. A thread or a trace of true memory may run anyhow through the roughest palimpsest or action painting. Into the ever-changing, multicolored waters moving, endless and inexorable, to the cliff's edge a true line may be sunk.

Marilyn herself was and is a fiction and an icon. Dayglo-bright in memory. In the elevator of the General Brock Hotel, going down, the operator said to her, "Miss Monroe, your blouse is unbuttoned." "Honey," she said, "it's supposed to be." It is reliably reported that as she bent over that day one milky-white breast popped out of that blouse and into the public domain.

A publicity poster for the film depicts her lying on her side atop the curved Canadian horseshoe falls. Her flesh is spilling out at us like water, like milk struck from a magic rock, inviting, uncontainable. She is goddess here too. She is queen of sexual magic, that pagan torrent. Red lips, a red dress. Puritan America's doomed sacrificial Aphrodite laid on cold Canada.

A myth, an illusion, you say — underneath which we now know there was a lost soul, a damaged waif, an angry bitch who wasn't strong enough, a wanton girl-child longing to be loved, perfectly: victim of America's inner wars.

The barbed-wire slit through my eyelid: an almost military image. I was crawling under a barbed-wire fence, there was a war on, perhaps I wanted to participate.

The blood ran down my face. I could not see out of one eye, I was half blinded by war.

The local Indians were called by historians the "Neutrals" because they tried to stay out of the wars between the larger Huron and Iroquois nations. The Neutrals controlled the only portage by the waterfall. For their pains they were completely wiped out by the Iroquois in the seventeenth century.

As early as A.D. 1000 there were Indian villages at the falls and along the river. These people grew corn, beans, and pumpkins, and even planted fruit trees. They fished for salmon and sturgeon in the gorge, and they hunted turkeys and other wildfowl on the heights above.

Jean de Brébeuf visited them in 1641. He noted:

> They embroider their robes with much care and industry and try to ornament them in divers fashions. They also make figures upon their bodies from head to foot with charcoal pricked into their flesh ... so that we see their faces and breasts figured like the helmets and cuirasses of soldiers in France.

Brébeuf attempted to convert these resplendent, charcoal-tattooed Neutrals to Christianity, but they preferred their own gods — spirits of wind, rain, sun, and forest. And, of course, Hinu or Hinun the thunder-god, who lived in his cave within the falls.

There is the legend, possibly spurious, of a maiden who was sacrificed to the mighty thunderer. Perhaps, then, Marilyn and Hinun belong in the same myth. Beauty and the Beast at the magic waterfall.

Sometimes I imagine myself at the edge of that Indian village. With the almost invisible dark people who are so used to the voice of the thunderer that they no longer always hear him. Their small fires shining in dusk. "I hear their broken consonants," as the poet said, like a murmuring of waters within waters.

When there was only forest and sky and cliff and river. One might stand gazing at the cataract. Listening.

When there were no wax museums, and there was

no giant Ferris wheel turning and turning like a reminder of the cyclical futility of industrial history.

Now the cars stream along the parkway in the summer dusk. A gleaming stream of metal-clad humanity, as Rupert Brooke might say. By day they seek out the rainbow, by night the artificial, garish colored lights projected on the falls. This is pure Hollywood even without Monroe. A stimulus to "love", whether in a cave, a car, or a pink motel. This is the city of cut-rate dreams. A tawdry slut made up to take advantage of the glamorous kindness of twilight.

Above the park is the real city — an overgrown village, rundown and seedy. A place where sullen youths dream of that spurious glamor. As if the falls itself were the gateway to America. To excitement, fulfilment of one's vaguest or most deceptive adolescent wishes. There is a continual roaring on the air that promises, promises. . . . It blends with a collective youthful sign of longing.

The boys and girls of this odd border-town play on both sides of the river. They play at love, they play at fantasy. At all the glistering illusions of youth.

This play — for me — is memory. . . .

THREE

◆

At university in Toronto, a year later, Ron succeeded, more or less, in forgetting about Buffalo and Felicia, her murdered brother, and the despairing note from Larry, who ran away and was never found by the police. Ron did not go back to Buffalo after the fatal night. He and Felicia corresponded for a while but then she didn't write any more. He was probably relieved.

Steve did not go to university. Instead, he knocked up his girlfriend and married her. Ron's father got him a job at the chemical company.

Carl went to California.

Ron went to Toronto, where there were people he could talk to about subjects other than sex and hockey. He decided there that he would specialize in history and English. He was soon happily involved in campus life.

Everybody was playing Elvis records. (He thought: maybe I even knew him in 1943. Memphis: a photo of several small white boys in white cotton shirts and shorts.)

Carl came home that summer with a red convertible sports car, a Triumph. And stories.

"Man, the chicks there. Like you wouldn't believe."

Carl was very tanned now, a golden boy.

"Like one night last fall I'm on the cable car on the hill in Frisco just looking around and there's this chick sitting opposite me. All of a sudden just like that she says, wanna go to a party, so I said why not, and there I am in a house full of blaring music and really gorgeous broads, natural blondes, and couples are retiring to the bedrooms. So I'm looking around for the girl who brought me and I can't find her and this other chick comes up and says, wanna dance, or shall we just go upstairs and ball. . . .

"God, you wouldn't believe the thirteen-year-old girl who said to me one day, like man, I'm deeply into balling right now. A real wild child. Balling, they call it. She said her mother was a whore. I tell you, at Berkeley anybody can get laid. Even Benson here. . . .

"And the beach. Though it rains a lot and there's smog like you wouldn't believe. But you can drive to Big Sur. It's gorgeous. . . .

". . . and this stunned broad she says to me, eh?, why *not* drink and screw and go to the races all night and day? Some day there'll be an earthquake, everybody says so, or else they'll drop the bomb on California out of jealousy, everybody says there's gonna be a war. . . ."

Ron admitted that Toronto was never like that.

". . . and the bitch wouldn't take off her pants and I blew my load all over her stomach, but that kind of reluctance is rare. . . ."

Ron wondered if it was all true. Steve said soberly that being married had its advantages too.

". . . after my old man agreed to help me buy the car, because man you're paralysed without wheels there, I took this chick for a drive up the coast. And we saw this flying saucer, I swear it, real close. It was a huge round light over the water. Christ, we were scared to death. We parked there and huddled together and watched the thing for half an hour. We couldn't move, it was as if it was controlling us. Finally it just moved away. Up and out over the ocean. I don't know what it was. They say the American air force has all kinds of things they won't talk about. Man, I was so amazed that I didn't even want to ball any more. . . ."

Ron had a summer job running the elevator at Table Rock House. The elevator took you down to the tunnels behind and underneath the falls. The lair of the thunder-god, according to the original Indians of the area. The kingdom of the dead, he might have called it, had he recalled his youthful interest in mythology. But the job was too dull to romanticize. Even the great falls, with colors shifting and changing according to the weather, was something you got used to.

Outside, at lunch time, he could see at a little distance the girls in the tourist booth further up along the park's grounds. They wore crisp white blouses and gave advice to tourists. From a distance they looked interesting.

One lunch-time he was dozing on the grass. He had been out late with Steve and Carl the night before.

He felt a foot prodding him. "Fuck off," he mumbled, thinking it was one of the teenage kids who put raincoats and rubber boots on the tourists. There was laughter. Female laughter. He opened his eyes.

It was one of the girls from the tourist booth. He sat up and looked at her.

"I thought I knew you," she said, smiling.

"It's you," he said stupidly.

"My name is Lisan," she said.

"Lisan?"

"I changed it."

But she hadn't changed. More assured, perhaps, but she had looked assured the first time he had seen her.

"I had to get away from Buffalo," she continued, "so I took off to New York, where I worked for a while. I did some modeling, using just the name Lisan, but I'm not skinny enough to make big money. And I got sick of the place. This spring I came back up this way. Then I came over to Canada to see if I could get a job here. I like moving."

"What about your parents?"

"I couldn't face them. They've never understood any of it. I can't help them now."

She was stretched out on the grass beside him. It was curiously intimate. She had good legs below her knee-length navy-blue skirt. She looked proper, ladylike, in a white blouse.

"It was good of you," she said, "to help me out that awful night."

"What else could I do?"

"You could have just left. As it was, you had quite a time persuading the police that you had no connection."

"I didn't come back again," he interrupted. He didn't like to remember the police grilling. It hadn't been pleasant.

"I didn't think you would."

"I should have."

"You should do what you want, I always do."

The same cool arrogance. Perhaps a cover for insecurity? He didn't know.

"Anyhow," she said, "I have to go back now. Come and

talk to me at lunch-times. We'll get to know each other after all."

"They never caught him," he mused. "If there'd been a trial I'd have had to go back for the trial."

"Did you know," said Lisan, sitting on the grass looking up from her official tourist-information booklet, "that in 1902 a woman named Alice Colie, from Buffalo, just like me, jumped into the falls?"

"Happens all the time."

"She wrote a note to her fiancé that read, 'Goodbye Ray, Mama, Papa, and all the dear ones. Do not think I do not love you, for I do. The waters are calling me.' Isn't that something?"

"Sounds like she wasn't ready to get married," said Ron.

"Don't be funny."

"Seriously," he said, "there are suicides all the time, they're just not reported, and certainly not stressed in the tourist brochures. But if you're at all that way inclined, then the place is hypnotic."

"I thought you were joking before."

"No you didn't."

"Then what about the people who go over in barrels? Are they flirting with suicide?"

"Some of them, probably. I think Red Hill must have been." Red Hill had died just a few years before.

"There's a whole family of Hills. It says here."

"Yeah. They call themselves river rats and they know everything there is to know about the river. They've rescued any number of foolish would-be stunters, and recovered the bodies of suicides because they know exactly where to look for them. But Red Hill Jr., in spite of this, insisted on going over the falls in a bunch of rubber tubing, canvas straps, and fish-netting. It was crazy."

"He killed himself?"

"Of course. The thing was half wrecked even before it got to the brink of the falls. He was done for."

"I can understand her," Lisan said. "To move as perfectly, as freely, as those waters. . . ."

On Ron's day off she phoned.

"I've rented a car," she said. "Come with me to the beach."

They were flying into cool, moving air.

"You're the only person I can talk to. Those girls are nitwits."

"Don't some of them go to university?"

"What's that got to do with it? God. Have they led boring lives!"

Then she said, "I suppose you're going back to college in the fall."

"Yes."

Silence.

"You've been on your own for some time now," he observed.

They were breezing along in the large convertible Lisan had rented for the day. She had insisted on driving even though she was, by her own admission, a fast, careless driver.

"I don't want a protector. My brother was a little too protective."

They hadn't brought towels or blankets. Both wore

bathing-suits under their clothes. They undressed quite casually together.

There weren't a great many people at the beach this weekday. Ron and Lisan stayed in the water for half an hour, then came out to dry in the sun.

"I suppose we should really have brought a blanket," she said. Her black hair was dripping water onto his shoulder as they sat side by side. He began to feel, quite irrationally, that strange as she was to him, he had known her always.

They sat without speaking, looking at the water.

When they were dry she said casually, "Let's go for a walk back in among the trees."

He looked at her.

She smiled. "You don't suppose I brought you all the way out here just to swim, do you?" she said. He did not know if she was joking or not.

They walked up to where there was grass instead of sand and then into the trees, holding hands. Taking her hand had seemed to Ron the thing to do under the circumstances.

The wood, if it was a wood, thickened. Then they came to a little grassy space, more or less enclosed, green, a pattern of light and shadow moving slightly in the breeze. "Here," she said as if recognizing the place.

They stood together, their bare bodies streaked with light and shade. Their hands unlinked.

Lisan's one-piece suit displayed an abstract pattern that resembled blue and red roses. Calmly she unzipped it at the back. He noticed now for the first time that she wore thin metal bracelets on both delicate wrists. There was birdsong all around them.

She pulled her suit down and off her legs expertly. Then came to him. They put their arms around one another. He had had scarcely a moment to observe her small breasts, flat stomach, her triangle of hair, her smooth thighs. Now he *felt* her whole body. He felt himself responding. They stood for a moment in a kind of underwater space of light and shade.

"I suppose," she said, scarcely breaking the spell, "that this is the first time for you."

"No. But it's the first time that matters."

She shuddered a little in his arms then, as if having second thoughts, hesitating. He stroked her back and then caressed her perfect buttocks.

Then he laid her down on the grass gently, his arm under her neck and shoulders. With his other hand he touched her breasts, her belly. Between her legs.

She pulled him toward her. Resisting for a moment, he pulled his trunks awkwardly down with his free hand. Then lowered himself over her. With her own free hand she guided him in.

Her hands moving on his back, his buttocks. The metal bracelets cool on his skin. The birds chattering, singing. That was what he remembered afterwards.

"Where do you live anyway?"

"Come and see."

They were driving back. Ron was driving. She had always refused to tell him where she lived till today.

She had a room in somebody's run-down house on Second Avenue. The landlord and his wife were out at work. Ron wanted to make love again right then and there on the bed, but Lisan said that they might come back any time now. The door had no lock.

"We can come here at lunch-time tomorrow," she said.

"Only separately. People will think you've got a room here too if you come and go alone."

They went out and had hamburgers at a diner. The world seemed unnaturally bright to him, even the sleazy diner had taken on a weird glamor. As if they had embarked upon a voyage, an adventure. Everything seemed to be moving so fast. Yet Lisan was as cool as usual.

"Let's go over the river and have a drink." she said.

"We're even legal there," Ron said happily. They were each twenty years old. The right age for love, surely, in whatever country.

She could read his mind, it seemed.

"Don't get too carried away," she said, smiling her peculiarly detached smile.

At Marty's they sat in a booth and drank Scotch. They could see out the window into the street.

"You know," said Lisan, "I haven't felt so relaxed since before — well, you know, before my brother — got killed. You relax me. I have to give you that."

"Maybe it's because I was there. There's no secret with me to make you tense."

"Secret? It's true I don't tell people right off the bat. But Angelo's death isn't a secret. I have better ones anyhow." She looked cool again.

"Is that an invitation to ask?"

"No."

"This lady has a secret," he said ironically.

"We all have secrets," said Lisan.

"There's Carl," said Ron, surprised. Carl was getting out of his sports car with a flashy blonde.

"Who's Carl?"

"He was with me the night I met you."

"I don't remember the others."

"It was almost two years ago."

Carl and his date came in. He spotted them immediately and came over.

"Well! Mind if we join you?"

"Why not?" said Ron automatically.

They sat down.

"Aren't you the mysterious Buffalo gal," asked Carl, "in Ronnie's past?" Ron thought that Carl had perhaps had a couple of drinks already.

"And who are you?" returned Felicia-Lisan.

"I'm Carl from California. And this is Mary-Jane. Mary-Jane, my old high-school buddy Ron."

"I've never been to California," said Lisan.

Mary-Jane said hello. She looked more shy than flashy close up. She was a peroxide blonde, an ordinarily pretty girl trying to look like Marilyn Monroe. Lisan's natural coloring made her seem a bit plastic.

"I'm Lisan," she said. Ron wondered then if she was wondering what he might have said to Carl about her either recently or in the past.

"They never caught old Larry, did they?" said Carl.

"No," she said coldly.

"Larry the murderer," said Carl.

"Maybe not," said Lisan, surprising Ron. "It might have been suicide. Or somebody else did it, and Larry found him that way. They never quite decided what."

"I didn't know that," said Ron.

A silence. Then Carl, finally embarrassed, began to speak of recent movies that he and Mary-Jane had seen. Mary-Jane now became less shy, and expressed a few opinions. Jayne Mansfield was a cow, not like the real thing. Elizabeth Taylor was not her type. That Marlon Brando

was really sexy. Paul Newman was almost as sexy. To Ron
and Lisan she seemed a likeable idiot, vulnerable, eager to
please.

Lisan wanted to go. So they excused themselves, leav-
ing Carl and Mary-Jane to their Californian fantasies.

"I'm sorry Carl went on about Larry. I never told him
more than the bare facts."

"I don't care what you told him. He's a creep."

Ron's lunch-hours became more interesting. They
would arrive separately on bicycles at Second Avenue.
Make love. Doze in Lisan's narrow bed. Wake to make love
again. Return separately, never late for work. Hungry
enough suddenly to buy chocolate bars and consume them
on the job.

"Do you know why I took you to that particular spot?"

"To make love."

"But why there?"

"You knew it?"

"Yes."

She was lying partly against, partly on top of him with
just a sheet over them.

"I had been there before," she said, "with my first
lover."

"Did you love him?"

"Yes, unfortunately. I couldn't refuse him anything."

"Should you have?"

She shifted away from him.

"I mean, if you loved him."

"I was only twelve years old."

He was shocked. But he wanted to seem sophisticated.

"So you really have been older than your age."

"I'm sorry I mentioned it. I'll tell you about it another time."

"All right."

He could not resist one more question.

"Have you taken anybody else there? I mean, of course you may have had lovers, that's not my business, but at that place?"

"No. Only you," she said. "And him. I've only been there twice."

"How do you know it was the same place? I mean, that exact place?"

She sat up then and looked down at him scornfully.

"Are you always so literal-minded? Is that what university does to you?"

They went to the beach again one day with Carl and Mary-Jane. Lisan and Ron sat up in dangerous exhilaration on the back of the sports car, holding on to one another, their legs bent down on either side of Mary-Jane in the front seat, Lisan's dark hair trailing out behind her in the wind. "Goodness," Mary-Jane said in her Marilyn Monroe voice, "I feel as if I ought to hold on to all your ankles." Carl was pleasanter and less smart-alecky this time. Lisan even laughed at some of his jokes. At the beach Mary-Jane confessed after a certain amount of teasing about her bleached hair that she had wanted to be exactly like Marilyn Monroe, but now realized that she wasn't sure who she really was. "Maybe Marilyn isn't either," said Lisan shrewdly. "Look at the childhood she had." Then Carl said something facetious, as usual. He made fun constantly of his summertime girl, so that Lisan and Ron were pleasant and patient with her almost as a consolation.

In August Lisan grew visibly restless. She no longer wanted to spend every lunch-time at Second Avenue. Their dalliance had by then become a bit routine, even Ron felt that. And they had run out of interesting things to do in the evening. He didn't have a car, he couldn't afford one if he was to save money. In any case one night-spot over the river was much like another after a while. A wanderer, she was becoming tired of this place, and he could sense it. Perhaps tired of him too. What did she really feel about him, he wondered.

"We ought to go somewhere," she said. "I'm fed up with this job. I've got a little money now."

"I have to save as much as I can," said Ron.

"To go to college," she said sardonically.

"University," he corrected.

Another day he said, "Why don't you get a job in Toronto this fall? It's a big city, there's a lot we can do together there."

"It's Hicksville," she said. She knew nothing about Toronto, he knew.

"It's changing," he protested. But he knew that all his friends in Toronto had spent their teenage years running off to Buffalo too.

"Well," he said, "maybe we could take a trip together in September before I go back."

"I'd like that," she allowed.

One day Carl dropped by to visit them as they ate their lunch on the grass. They admired once again his classic sports car.

"Take you for a spin," he said to Lisan.

"Why not?"

"Go ahead," said Ron. "I'll read my book."

"Books, books," muttered Lisan cheerfully.

They were gone for half an hour. Lisan was almost late for work.

One day, a week later, she didn't come to work at all. She had been a little strange for days now. At lunch-time Ron went up to Second Avenue. He had a duplicate of her front-door key. Now, not knowing what he might find, he used it. There was nobody home downstairs, thank God. Her room was unlocked, of course. There were other roomers, but none of them came home at noon.

She wasn't there. Her bed had been slept in.

I'll just stay here, he thought recklessly, until she comes home. He would have it out with her. Why couldn't she come to Toronto? If she wouldn't, what were they going to do? Weekend trips back and forth? Or was she just bored with him already? He felt somehow that he had very little claim on her, even though they were lovers. But he was determined to press the issue. She had been around so much. He had to persuade her that he loved her, that he could give her a security different from anything she had known. He had a weird certainty about this. He could persuade her that he loved her.

Did he love her? He could not think about this for long. He needed her.

He went downstairs and phoned Table Rock House, telling them he wasn't feeling well. Perhaps they believed him. One of the guys from the cloakroom could run the elevator.

Lisan's temporary room held only the narrow bed, a bookcase full of the landlord's departed son's old paperbacks, a broken-down easy chair, and a lamp. There were no longer any pictures on the walls.

He sat up on her bed, his running-shoes off, reading a battered copy of *A Portrait of the Artist as a Young Man*. But his concentration wasn't good. The style defeated him even as it intrigued him. Once the phone rang downstairs but he didn't dare answer it.

From where he sat he could see the street outside the window. A tree, sidewalk. Bright sunlight and intense shadow. It was an oddly familiar scene. Just a few streets away, he thought, his mother would be occupying herself in some way, doing housework or watching the afternoon soap operas, in the Benson family's somewhat similar house. Last spring his brother had married and departed.

At four o'clock Carl's red Triumph, with Carl and Lisan in it, pulled up out front. They had what seemed to him a long conversation. He could only catch the odd word. Once she laughed heartily. A little while after that she got out and Carl drove off. They didn't kiss.

He heard her on the stairs. Thank God Carl hadn't come in too, he couldn't have handled that. As it was, it was bad enough.

She came in the door. Then stopped abruptly.

"What in hell are you doing here?"

"Waiting for you. Where did you take off to?"

"I suppose you saw us out the window," she said. "Just this morning I looked out right from where you are now and there he was, car and all."

"You didn't have to go with him."

"It was a change," she said evenly. "We went to Buffalo, so I could look around. I haven't been there for a long time. It was rather sad."

"To Buffalo. Not to the beach."

"Of course not."

"I thought you said Carl was a creep."

"Only superficially. He's your friend, isn't he?"

"I thought so."

"Look, it had nothing to do with you." Then, more evenly: "It occurred to me that you might come here and wait for me."

"What about me?"

"A good question. Aren't you going back to university?"

"What if I don't?"

"I don't believe you," she said.

"You're so bloody cool about everything."

She sat down beside him on the bed and began to unbutton his shirt.

"All that traveling," she said, "has made me a bit horny."

He was shocked that she used the word "horny".

"I need it," she said. "It was bad going back there."

They were sitting on the grass at lunch-time.

Ron said: "Let's be honest with each other. When I go back to Toronto then for you it's over?"

"Yes," she said.

"Why?"

"I'm too restless to settle down. Yet. Maybe some time, maybe even you. But I want to see more, do more. This summer has been good, it was probably what I needed for a while. You've been good. But come fall I have to go."

To California? He would not say it.

"Look," she said, "I think we should cool it off now. We've had a nice time. Let's stay friends. But no more trips to Second Avenue."

"I'm officially cut off," he said sarcastically.

"Don't be crude. Don't spoil it."

All her conversation today had sounded rehearsed to him.

Ron and Carl now avoided one another. They didn't phone, they didn't meet by arrangement or by accident.

There came the inevitable day. Carl, who did not have a job and who had never had to work very hard at anything — not because his parents were especially affluent but because they doted on their only son and paid his bills — cruised by at lunch–hour. Ron saw him stroll up to the tourist booth. He saw Lisan drive off with him.

Laboriously riding his bicycle up the hill through the cut and into the city proper, Ron despised himself. But he had to see with his own eyes what he knew perfectly well.

The red sports car was parked, triumphantly, in front of the house on Second Avenue. With Carl, Lisan flaunted their togetherness — no sneaking in separately. But of course (he saw) she was about to leave, so she didn't care what anybody thought now.

Worst of all, he *saw* them. In his mind's eye he saw them making love, their lithe, naked bodies moving together on the narrow bed. Entwined, her legs wrapped around him. Her pale skin, his fine gold hair. . . .

He knew that he would always see them like that.

"Yes, I'm going. I'm sorry."
"When?"
"Saturday."
"Saturday."

"I'm quitting tomorrow. He says he doesn't mind going back early. He loves it there."

"Do you love him?"

"I like him."

They were standing at the railing just above the falls.

"I have to move on. I can't explain it or justify it. I go crazy if I stay put too long. Can you understand?"

He thought he understood. It was how he had felt the night he met her. But somehow his restlessness had taken him on a different path. For he had gone to university. And by and large loved it. It had been an intellectual liberation — an escape from this mindless, roaring city. A different journey from hers. A different way to the same freedom? Perhaps. Or maybe it was simply that she had the guts to be truly free of convention and expectation, and he didn't. Her existence challenged him.

Around them were numbers of other couples and groupings of other people with all the rhythms of their "other", mysterious lives. All poised at this brink, drawn to it. Because of the white–water noise they could not hear Lisan's and Ron's low, urgent voices. Photographs were being taken. Behind Lisan the ever-changing waters pursued their heedless course, a mingled roar of voices returning from beyond the brink. Gaiety at the edge, gallows humor.

"I won't take money from him. I'll get a job there. We'll have a good time and then go our separate ways. He's like that anyway, isn't he?"

"And that's what you want?"

"It's what I want now."

He was at last too angry, angry with himself too, to reply. He turned and walked away. She did not at first follow him.

Ron took Mary-Jane to the movies. They saw *Vertigo*, the latest Hitchcock. It begins with a man falling to his death from a high rooftop in San Francisco. It features those steep, sinister streets. Streets that Carl must have roamed. It's about being haunted. Ron liked it. But Mary-Jane, missing the point, thought Kim Novak too cold to be much of a rival to Monroe. And she couldn't follow the plot. Yet the film upset her because she had always been terrified of heights. Terrified of falling. Afterwards she talked for a long time about Carl. He was the neatest guy she had ever met. She thought she was in love with him. She thought that the affair with Lisan would not last and that next summer he would come back to her. Lisan was too cold for him. He would learn to appreciate his Mary-Jane, she was sure of it. She would wait for him. She had her job at Woolworth's. All those California girls were too shallow for him finally, he had told her this. He would come back. She would forgive him. But she was very unhappy now. It was hard. She invited Ron into her house, her parents were out at a party. So he screwed her on the living-room sofa, which creaked loudly. She was quite passive throughout, unlike Lisan. Afterwards she cried.

A huge postcard from the road. A picture of the Grand Canyon.

Hi Ron,
  I didn't have the guts to say goodbye to you. I snuck out of the room to do this. You must think I'm a bastard. I've never moved in on a friend's girl before. But I love her. I couldn't help it, I never met anyone like her. (All's fair in love and war. Right? Right?) I don't know what I'm saying. Believe me, I

never loved a girl before. I'm terrified I can't hold
on to her. She says you're a good person.

Carl

Ron wondered bitterly if postal workers and postmen
read the cards to lighten the monotony of their daily lives.
Fortunately he had picked up the mail this morning before
either of his parents thought to do so.

FOUR

◆

How to continue this story? I have briefly reconstructed scenes and events that I can no longer recall with a first clarity. (Others I have certainly forgotten altogether.) I have done this with a certain coldness — the better to examine what becomes, increasingly, a painful experience. But what, beyond pain, have I retained? What do I understand now about this story?

Not as much as I would like. I remember details. Events. I have some new thoughts about them. I ask myself yet again what, "really", happened.

Remembered "facts". That Lisan and young Ron became, technically, at some point (I honestly don't, incredible as it may seem, remember where or when sex first occurred, it just did), lovers, and that they spent some little time that summer with Carl and Mary-Jane. As I have presented him, Carl must seem, I realize, rather shallow — but there was a thoughtful if somewhat cynical side to him too. He was self-indulgent but not a fool. As for Mary-Jane, she was playing a role that did not suit her. Who she really was I do not know even now, for I lost track of her after she left the city and do not know what became of her in later years. Probably she is a respectable matron in Pittsburgh, or some place like that, whose children are white-collar workers; all of them voted for Ronald Reagan in 1980 and 1984.

Lisan and Ron were children playing at love. They did not really know one another very well. For him, easy and fairly frequent sex was a new and exhilarating experience to be savored. For her he was, perhaps, a diversion, though also a temporary haven. Her restlessness was temporarily assuaged. So they enjoyed one another for a time. But this lucky equilibrium could not, in the nature of things at the waterfall's edge (and elsewhere), last very long.

It did not last very long.

Teenage romance, betrayal — the stuff of old ballads and of many silly popular songs then and later. These four are not quite teenagers, of course; they are very young adults. Feeling their way. Between childhood and some distant, unanticipated species of maturity. Between great and lesser wars.

There is a blessing on youth, even on its darkest moments of acute unhappiness. Every emotion, experience — good or bad — is so sharp, unambiguous. It can burn in the brain. In youth one savors pain as much as pleasure; later all is dulled, a little or a lot, by attrition, and too much of life, good or bad, pleasant or painful, is also sadly predictable.

Perhaps that is why it is better to have loved and lost than never to have loved (i.e., experienced love — of anyone, anything — in pleasure and pain, with that first acute, searching intensity) at all. Even if such intensity should later seem illusory, it is still of infinite value.

What happened begins to seem inevitable when one is older. As if there had been no alternatives. Memory selects acute moments, makes patterns of them, often reorganizing events and sequences to do so. This is the origin of fiction. Memory (all unconsciously) plays, refracts, composes. As the sunlight and the fine mist endlessly rework, reweave Noah's rainbow (it arches and wavers there) over babbling, tumbling, dancing-green waters.

Indeed, as I look back (or down) on him, young Ron seems like someone else. Though I think I understand him now. His uncertainties generated arrogance; he could not manage grace or resignation — let alone acceptance or reconciliation with the world. He was, I was, too fluid. So I tried to *seem* certain, solid. At that time.

I decided then at university that my high school years at home had been a long sleep. I had been more alive to the world, I thought, as a small child. If I had weathered most of the storms of adolescence with outward stolidity, it was probably because of my friend Steve, who was steady and stolid by nature, and who would probably be exactly the same thoroughly reliable person at ninety that he had been at nine. Other boys, uncertain in their adolescence, had been attracted to him, an informal gang had even formed around him, for that reason. But my own apparent stolidity, originally borrowed (I guess) from Steve, was largely fake, in spite of my own stolid father. It was a mask or a lid to keep down the numerous people I could sense agitating inside me. I had wanted to *be* everyone and this had frightened me. Or else I was nobody, a blank mirror that reflected those around me. I "caught" other people's emotions. I had to protect myself. So I had opted for a time to "be" Steve. But that would no longer do.

Carl had brought out another side of me — a careless, joking, somewhat nihilistic humorist. "Sick transit." Suspended between Steve and Carl, I had lived out my adolescence fairly safely, with only the two episodes of Felicia-Lisan to disturb me into an awareness of my own insufficiency, my own incompleteness. But she left me, and she left me (I thought then) nothing.

So at university I opted for the arts and the intellect. This would be my new haven, my refuge. In a way — though I was not entirely conscious of it at the time — what I was doing was defining myself *against* Carl (as well as against Lisan, which was more obvious). For I knew even then that though Carl was intelligent, he perversely denied himself the disciplines of human study and art. He refused to believe in the virtue of these things, he was a cynic. Consequently, he would fritter away his life in pleasure, believing the worst of the world. Hemingway, the romantic nihilist and hedonist par excellence, was the only writer I remembered him to have read with approval. Now that he was studying mathematics in California he probably read no serious literature at all.

I felt, naively but not altogether erroneously, that university had reawakened my mind and sensibility, that it had taken me forever away from the world of my slumbering parents, from their mere plodding persistence in life, and — even more important — away from that frontier of nightmare life-in-death with all its false excitement and false glamor: I mean the border city where I had grown up. I would live now, I convinced myself, entirely in the world of great civilizations, poetry, intellectual quest.

And yet I think I knew without ever quite admitting it that this haven would not suffice, could not really keep me safe. Yes. I think young Ron knew this, somehow even at that time.

FIVE

◆

(As the lights dim one sees Carl in a sordid room in San Francisco. At the rear of the stage is an alcove with a view of the blue bay in the distance. In the bay is the island prison of Alcatraz. But as the lights dim, this prospect, which is both charming and sinister, along with the details of the room, fades away, until only Carl, sprawled on an old, collapsed, dirty sofa, is spotlit. He is gaunt, thinner than we have seen him. His eyes have deep shadows under them.)

CARL:

Porking Jane Berners in a field. Is that what it's all about? Is that all I *remember* about that place?

Whatever happened to her?

Funny. I remember the smell of the grass. Nothing much else. A rank smell. Jane saying: First you have to say you love me because there has to be some love. Doesn't there? What a laugh that was.

How many times with her? She was fat but she was first.

At this moment I actually remember her better than any

of the others. The beauties. The goddam beauties. . . .

Is she still doing sixteen-year-olds?

"The guys." All desperately wanting to get laid.

Sex is, they say, not at all the most efficient means of biological reproduction. Asexual reproduction is far superior — having *two* sexes is cumbersome.

Sex must be partly a joke — like the universe.

We used to call her tits "big burners". We called her a pig but we knew she was reliable. She would put out for most anybody. Her cunt was home base for all the boys of summer.

That field of long grass was, you might say, a kind of womb. The strong smell from the Shredded Wheat factory. Steve and Ron and Larry. The guys. We all jerked off together there once — during recess. That must have been in Grade Eight. Funny. I had totally forgotten about that. For years and years. But this stuff brings back the oddest early memories.

The Rogers sisters. Tough broads from Centre Street. Not twins, but in the same grade. Mouthy, loud. One was almost pretty, the other hatchet-faced. Killed in a car crash? I seem to know that. When? In high school maybe. That time in Grade Six when Betty Rogers beat up Larry. She challenged him to a fight. He was totally humiliated.

Betty had a crush on Steve. He was already the school's baseball hero. He may have done her once or twice later on too.

He wouldn't talk about it. I think he felt sorry for her. A fucking gentleman.

She didn't even finish Grade Eight.

All I can remember right now are those early years. Why? I wanted like hell to get away from that place all during that time.

Larry ran away. God. Isn't it something that *he* was the

one who actually left? Now he . . . I don't want to think about that.

I guess we were always who we are. Larry was just born queer. Steve is the athlete, the hero type, not over-endowed with grey matter. Ron. The intellectual? Maybe he was always some kind of poet. Too sensitive for his own good.

He's got a mean streak, though, too. Like me. Maybe that's why we were friends. We were incredible brats. Bombing the cars from the top of the cut. Steve would never have descended to that kind of thing, he was just too much of a Boy Scout. Larry would, though. He'd have loved it — the sadistic, perverted bastard.

Ronnie cut open his eyelid with barbed wire. He had to wear an eyepatch for weeks. Everybody thought he was interesting for a while. Like a pirate. My father sewed it up. On the kitchen table or something. He came home and said to my mother, these kids, they do the damnedest things to themselves. So she got even more worried than usual about me. Didn't want me going to "the cut" any more. But Ronnie's cut wasn't serious. It healed over quickly. He never tried to crawl under that fence again.

My father. How he wanted me to be the doctor, lawyer, little businessman of the family. He should have had Steve for a son. He could have done something for *him*. My mother less ambitious, even rather lazy. Like me. Probably good in bed. What a thought. But . . . Yeah. I actually interrupted them once. When was that? It was ten o'clock or something, not that late, I suddenly wanted to go out, I wanted to know if I could take his car. I didn't have one yet. It was quite dark in their bedroom. But he was distinctly embarrassed. She said nothing at all — though I know she didn't want me going out. I guess that's why he let me take the car. They were so embarrassed.

I wanted to see that girl . . . what was her name?

Oh, I'm tired. . . .

I need . . .

I could phone . . .

No. I'm not *that* desperate.

Yet.

Cynthia. For Christ's sake. That was her name. Fucking Cynthia. Only we didn't quite get that far. I *did* see her that night. I was desperate for her body. She let me do most everything else. Said it amused her to see how excited I got. Cock-tease.

Are girls people? Or are they from some other planet?

God knows. I'll be brave. I'll admit it. After all the fucking — all the girls I've had — I don't think I understand women any better than I did when I was sixteen.

Jeez. How old am I? Christ, I'm not even sure. . . . Just now.

I should dry out. I really should. I *will*. Some time. . . . How can I have loved sex so much and not even particularly *like* women? Most women.

I liked my mother. All right. She was dumb but kind.

Hey. Maybe *that's* what I need.

Good lord. Mary-Jane. Old Mary-Jane. She was . . . She was damn like my mother.

Funny. I never thought about that before. I knew it, of course.

Now when was that? In high school? No. Later. It was . . .

It was after my first year here. I'd never had so much screwing as that "golden" year. But all the broads came and went, they were screwing anything that moved.

I got sick of American girls. At least the kind I met here. It was just too much of a good thing.

It all went by too fast. Not that I wanted to get married or anything. But I wanted to slow down a little. So I was actually relieved to go home for a while that summer.

So where did I meet her? I mean what's-her-name . . . Uhhh . . . Mary-Jane. Yeah.

I think it was in a store. Yeah. She worked in a store, I don't know why I went in there. She had very bleached hair, it made me think of Berkeley so I went over to talk to her.

She opened her legs on the second date. We were parked at the half-moon above the falls. She said "don't" and "oh" a few times but not very firmly. It was pretty uncomfortable, to say the least, we found better places afterwards. She wanted it, of course.

She wasn't a virgin. But she wasn't a slut either. She'd only had one previous prick stuck into her. Or so she said. I certainly believed her then.

She had dropped out of school. The other high school. If I'd ever seen her before, it would have had to be in her pre-blonde days when she was mousy and less well-developed. She had matured. Oh boy.

Then the silly bitch went and fell in love with me.

Well, to be honest, I suppose I wanted her to. I wanted it regular with one chick for a while. For a change. I suppose I treated her badly. But what's a guy supposed to do? A young horny guy? Go without? Masturbate? I mean, it wasn't like here, where a variety of pussy is pretty constantly available.

One night I tried to get her to go down on me. But she wouldn't. Otherwise she was all right. Not much of a mover and shaker but she liked it all right.

She used to sing in a Baptist choir on Sundays.

Mary-Jane. Old Mary-Jane. Hot dog. I haven't thought of her in years. I could get all sentimental. I wonder what in hell ever happened to her?

She got to be a drag, I recall. She got all serious — she

kept telling me how much she loved me. How she'd like to
have my *baby*. That was certainly pushing the panic button.
The girl wasn't too bright.

So I left her behind when I came back to California.
Said I'd write. Came back early to get away from that
situation. I . . .

Didn't I?

'Cause something else is nagging at me. . . .

Mary-Jane on her back. Spreading her thighs in the
moonlight in her fenced-in backyard. She had pale white
skin there like a true blonde, though she wasn't one. She
had lovely big tits. I used to like to play with them. Melons.
Not like . . .

No. Oh no.

I don't want to think about . . . I knew there was some
danger. . . .

Sneaky. Sneaking up on me. Like that. I should have
known Mary-Jane was just an excuse. . . .

Damn you, Carl. You led yourself right back to . . .
Following that bloody thread . . .

Lisan.

The bitch.

Just when I'd forgotten it all. When I was all caught up
in the life before.

Go back. Jane Berners, the field. *Louise Jones*. My God.
My *second* lay. She was, I told the guys (breathless with
curiosity), a natural redhead. I . . . .

Oh God.

It's too late. You've done it. Did it.

Lisan. Oh God, I loved her. I wanted her so desperately.
Was that my fault?

A series of goddam motel rooms. All exactly alike. In
the dark you forgot where you were. The changing expres-

sions on her face in the morning while she slept (it was the only time she betrayed any agitation).

I was guilty, of course. About Ron. And she had really liked him. So I was jealous too — I wanted her to *see* me. Even when we were making love I wasn't sure it mattered to her who I was. It made me slightly frantic, jumpy.

She was so cool.

As we got farther and farther from the falls I quieted down a lot, though. Ronnie began to seem a long way away then. And Mary-Jane — I knew I had hurt her badly too.

But I couldn't help myself. Could I?

I loved her.

I had never been in love before.

I never thought she would stay with me. I never thought I could hold onto her. But I hoped desperately.

By the Grand Canyon I thought of killing her, and then myself . . . or was that at Death Valley? More appropriate there.

I mean, just for a while when I was driving. She had fallen asleep. She was murmuring unhappily in her sleep. We were getting closer to Frisco. The end.

I mean, it was only a passing fantasy. The world seemed for a while so weird.

I didn't want the trip ever to end. What if we had just vanished?

We weren't in a rush. In the mornings we would often "sleep in", make love, talk — in that moving American motel we occupied each night, every room the same room, all the way from northern New York to California.

Love. It isn't the same as sex. (Says he, sagely.) But I was pretty cynical before.

When. . . .

I think it was that time we drove to the beach. In my car. Mary-Jane and I sitting down, Lisan and Ronnie perched on the back. I drove as fast as I could to give them a bit of a thrill.

I think all four of us were happy that day.

Why does nothing good last?

Why is there no balance?

That lasts. . . .

It's like the moment before the water goes on over the cliff. It seems to stop. It's glassy-smooth, beautiful then. Green glass. Time stops. Or seems to stop. Time *stretches* itself.

Lisan came out of the water dripping wet. Her long black hair wet. Lithe, almost boyish. She made Mary-Jane suddenly seem overdone, overblown. The sun on her shining black hair when she lay there on the sand.

I made love to Mary-Jane three times that evening. Seeing. . . .

In the desert I asked her to live with me when we got there. She said she had to be independent.

I can't bear to think much about what happened afterwards. The arguments. The weekends we sometimes spent. The dope we did. It all runs together now. I hit her once. *Did I? Oh God.* . . . The different apartments she had. I found her. I smashed a door down. Which one? That bruiser she had then bashed me one in the eye. I got stitches at emergency. I think they drove me there. That time.

And the girls who tried to pick up the pieces. California girls.

How did I end up here? Like this? How did it all happen? Larry. . . .

I can't. I just can't think. . . .

I need . . .

If she had loved me. . . .

If she had only just loved me. . . . Or . . .

Would it have been just the same anyway? That's the most horrible thought of all.

So here I am, strung out, as the song goes. All strung out. "A long way from home. . . ."

Take me back. To old Kentucky. No.

Take me back to Jane Berners and the green fields of childhood. Everything was simpler then.

Was it?

Whatever I did, I loved her.

Lisan, I *loved* you.

Before you, I was young. Now . . .

Now I try to find some other space so I can hold you at a distance. All of you. All of my life.

Some day I'll go too far out and drown. The waters will close over me. . . .

Some day the earthquake will strike again, the waters will rise up out of the bay, the ocean, and a great tidal wave will smash against this high-rise building and carry everything away. It will be the end. Good. . . .

I'm so tired. . . . So tired. When did I sleep? What day. . . .

(He is dozing off now. As the spotlight on him dims, the other lights gradually come up, revealing once again the shabby room and the distant prospect of bay and prison as Carl appears to sink more and more into the old, collapsed sofa whose stuffing is poking out in places.)

It wasn't all her fault. She had her own problems. Only I never knew what they were.

God knows where she is now.

Maybe I don't even care any more.

Maybe it was all a dream.

Maybe. . . . Tomorrow. I'll wake up out of this long dream. . . .

I don't . . .

Larry? Where . . . I'll . . .

Tired. . . . Too tired. . . .

SIX

◆

Ron was tortured by the thought that Lisan and Carl perhaps suited one another. They were both adventurers, trav-
elers. At other times he was sure that they would soon
break up. But he determined to put them out of his mind.
To concentrate on his studies.

He also went out with a succession of girls in Toronto.
He even slept with some of them. He told himself that he
was tough and cynical. Not vulnerable any more.

After a few months he assured himself: I'm over it. I
won't be "had" again. By anyone.

He was building a hard shell aroud himself, it
seemed. . . .

Once, years before, Carl and Steve had for a while
ignored and excluded Ron, not so much out of any very
active dislike (though they complained to each other that
he had gotten morose and "boring"), but because they had
entered a phase of close companionship in which, for a
time, they didn't much need other friends. Later on, when

they bought the car, there was a renewed gang sensibility, that which is still summed up by the enduring if not endearing beer-commercial tag "the boys". But for a time Carl and Steve were inseparable and exclusive. All that summer after the end of Grade Eight they kept to themselves.

Ron was hurt. He and Carl had been "best friends" even before they began to hang around Steve in public school. Now Ron felt he had been replaced, just as when his brother Mike had gone off to school ahead of him and developed other attachments.

He and Carl had competed, more or less unconsciously, for Steve's attention. Steve was the school's baseball hero. He had always before treated them equally. But now that Carl had won the competition, Ron felt betrayed. He resented Carl bitterly for a time. He resented Carl's effort-less ability to be entertaining. But he probably missed Carl, too, more than Steve, though he could not analyse it. He only knew he had been left behind.

One day he went over to Carl's house, though he knew he was not much wanted. Steve was there, of course. They greeted him without enthusiasm, if without obvious hos-tility. They seemed faintly superior, amused at his atten-dance on them. They're treating me the way they used to treat Larry when he was still hanging around, Ron thought bitterly. But he could not leave, even though he was humi-liated.

They were practicing basketball, passing and shooting at the basket in Carl's backyard. This was their obsession this summer. They wanted to make the high school team. Ron was not much good at basketball. But he took his turn, and even sank a couple of baskets. Carl and Steve were obviously not much impressed, though they com-mended him routinely.

"Well, I've gotta go," he said finally.

They did not object. As Ron left, Carl's father, Dr. Palmer, pulled into the driveway, and waved at him amiably. He was a friendly man. He had once sewn up Ron's eyelid, and was special for that reason.

The next evening Carl turned up at Ron's house.

"Want to go to the movies?"

"Where's Steve?"

"Baby-sitting his sister." Ron knew that Carl would normally be there too. He didn't think Steve and Carl ever spent an evening apart these days. Probably Carl would go and see the movie again with Steve.

"Don't do me any favors."

"Don't be so touchy. Don't you want to see the blonde Californian beast's tits again?"

So they went.

The somewhat older Ron wanted to put himself beyond such humiliation. Especially after Carl and Lisan had betrayed him. So at university he allowed no one to get too close to him. He treated his girlfriends casually, which seemed to make them all the more eager to please. This is it, he told himself then. This is the way you manage women. No more sad songs for me. I'm tough now. And outwardly he was.

Till the letter from his mother came.

Dear Ronald,

    I am not much of a correspondent as you know. But I feel I must tell you that I am very worried about your father. For a long time now he hasn't felt very well. Finally Dr. Palmer has seen him and he isn't sure just what is the matter. At least, he hasn't told me anything so far. Next week he is going into the hospital for tests.

I think it would be a good idea if you could come home for a few days. Michael and Lois were over for dinner on Tuesday but your father was very gloomy and withdrawn. I don't know what to do.

With love,
Mother

Damn. Why didn't she phone? Children of the Depression, Ron's parents considered long-distance calls an extravagance. His father could die, and she still wouldn't phone, he thought.

Dear Ronald,

They have now got the results of all the tests and have decided to operate on your father's liver. Do you remember how yellow he looked when you were here last week? That is because of a growth in his liver. They are going to operate this Friday, which is when I think you said your exams would be over. So I hope you will come home as soon as you are finished.

I am very worried, of course, but there is nothing we can do except wait and hope for the best. . . .

Ron went home on Thursday, not sure just what to expect. Or what to feel. He had not anticipated a family crisis. He arrived at the house, he went to the hospital in a state of mild shock. Everything at home seemed to be changing.

His mother might indeed be very worried, but he found her more lively than she had been in years. Something had finally broken. She fussed over her husband more energetically than ever now that it probably made no difference. Her life had been, it seemed, largely uneventful for some years. Since her youth, perhaps.

Harriet Listowel Benson was the daughter of a Presbyterian clergyman well established in Toronto. Widowed early in life, he had expected his only child to attend adult church services regularly from the age of ten, and from not long thereafter to teach children not much younger than herself in the Sunday school as well. Consequently she hated church, and ceased to attend after marrying Oswald Benson when she was twenty-four. Though her father had refused to send her to university, she had met and married a university graduate in defiance of his wishes. She insisted, of course, that her two sons receive religious instruction from the Lutheran church of her husband's family background but declined to attend it herself, her reasoning being that she was not a Lutheran, and that if she could not attend church with her husband she would not go to the Presbyterian church by herself either. As they grew older, even the boys understood that this was just an excuse. Since they disliked Sunday school and church just as much as she did, they quit too when they were teenagers — over her hypocritical (or perhaps guilty) objections.

Ozzie Benson, however, continued to go by himself to church, though not every Sunday. It was never clear to the rest of them whether he believed in any of what was proposed there or not. Possibly he just wanted to get out of the house. He was increasingly a man who kept most of his thoughts to himself.

Ron often wondered where his own intellectual bent and love of reading had come from. He supposed it had come from his mother's father. Neither of his parents read much. Nor did Mike.

When he was younger his mother was given to saying

things like "I wouldn't walk across the street to see Gracie Fields" or "I'm sick and tired of your whining" — expressions and idioms that had somehow vanished from her speech over the years. She had been a much more definite person with definite opinions once. Indeed, neither of his parents seemed to Ron to be quite the same person he thought he remembered from childhood. His father had withered into silence; his mother, once apparently so competent, now seemed merely fussy.

"*My* father," announced Ozzie Benson now from his hospital bed, "died of lung cancer at the age of forty-seven. When *I* was at university."

Ron had not known this. His grandfather, he knew, had worked for some years in his youth at the chemical company, but only in the factory. Later he left for Toronto to set up enterprises of his own. Most of these failed.

"Well, *you're* going to be all right," said Harriet brightly but without great conviction. All of the small family was gathered around. Lois, who was pregnant, was visibly upset.

The walls of the hospital room were painted a color that was either cream or pale yellow depending upon how the light fell. This color bothered Ron for some reason. Ozzie Benson's face was also yellow. It was a warm, sunny day. The new leaves were gold-green just outside the window. As if, he thought, after war and heavy atomic fall-out, all the world were slowly turning yellow. . . .

"Well, he certainly has the jaundice," said Mike as they left the hospital.

"They say the liver is blocked," said Harriet.

The operation took place the next morning. The surgeon removed a tumor from the liver. But the cancer had spread and there was nothing more that could be done

about it. It was only a matter of time. Dr. Palmer told
Harriet, who then told Mike and Ron.

The brothers were having a drink late at night. Harriet
had gone to bed, and Mike was in no hurry to go home to
his own house.

"I think," said Ron slowly, "that it's the chemicals that
did it to him. All those years in the lab."

"You would," said Mike bitterly, "have some such the-
ory. You've never dirtied your own hands at any real work,
dangerous or otherwise." He was a little drunk, Ron saw,
and certainly upset.

"Face it," Ron said. "It's possible."

"Anything's possible. They don't know what causes
cancer."

Ron was wondering if Mike and Steve were going to
suffer the same fate as his father. And grandfather. He was
sure it was the chemicals.

"He's had a difficult life," said Mike. "Though you
wouldn't know, you never paid any attention to him."

"They didn't seem to me to be living at all — these last
ten or more years."

"How would you know? Off with your asshole gang
all the time, and then in Toronto learning to be superior."

"You're just pissed off," said Ron, "because you've let
yourself get trapped at the company too."

The hostility between them was now in the open. Perhaps it had always been there waiting, but they had been
too busy with their individual lives to notice. They had
been close only for a while in childhood.

"I'm going home, I've drunk too much," said Mike —
the closest he would come to apology.

"You needed to," said Ron.

Ozzie Benson came home from the hospital and took up residence in the rocking-chair on the front porch. He did not go back to work. (Nor did he ever go to church again. The minister came to see him. Twice. But Ozzie disliked the man. Why had he gone to church all those years?) When Ron came home each day from his summer job as a customs officer on the bridge to the States — the "Rainbow Bridge" — his father would be waiting for him. They would sit on the front porch and drink beer. Now that he was dying, Ozzie didn't see any reason not to drink, nor did he care any more — though Harriet still did — what the neighbors might say. She did not dare to complain. By dying before her eyes he had finally silenced her.

The lilac tree in the front yard was coming into its brief glory of heaven-blue cluster blossoms. As a child Ron had been fascinated by this.

"I met your mother at a dance," said Ozzie. "She had told her father that she was going to visit a girlfriend because he didn't like her going to dances. He was very straitlaced, that man. I belonged to a hard-drinking fraternity but I told your mother that I never touched a drop, ho-ho. She was a pretty little thing, cute as a button. I used to take her to the movies. Her father didn't approve of movies either. We agreed that he was 'extreme'. It didn't really sink into me then that she was pretty strict herself."

They could hear the falls in the distance. Fragrance of lilacs. Does he smell it, Ron wondered.

"I don't suppose she's listening. I don't suppose it matters any more. But our biggest problem over the early years was that I had a whole lot more appetite than she did. If you know what I mean. She never did take to it. I brought her here, where I'd grown up, and she got along with everybody all right, but I don't think she has ever really cared for this town. Just for you kids, at least when you were small. After that there wasn't much for her. And all I had was the job, which had interested me at first, but that was a long time ago, I can tell you."

Ozzie talked nonstop now after years of silence. He talked not so much to his son Ron in particular as to that almost disinterested curiosity in Ron that acted as a screen for the projection of a life, or a self, the closest perhaps that Ozzie might now come to finding a listening God. Not that he likely thought in such terms, of course; he merely waited each day for Ron to appear so that he could resume his monologue. Calmly he reviewed his life, but with no hint of despair or any reaction of anger any stronger than momentary irritation. There had always been something passive about him, Ron saw now. He was at rest if his days had an order — once the American job, now the rocker on the porch as he grew weaker and weaker, and woozier and vaguer too from the pain-killers he took. The beer had no special effect on him, it was a comforter of sorts. He was making do, as always. It was not as if he had ever had or had now any notion of what a more meaningful work or marriage might have been like. His life had been what it had been, and now his death approached as it must, that was all. He had no imagination.

"Marriage is largely a habit, you know. Work is a habit. When I was at university I worked hard to get a degree. Oh, I was interested in chemistry too, but mainly it was a meal ticket. Well, I've always had a job till now. I gave my kids the necessities. What more is a man supposed to do?

"I suppose," he said, looking a little resentfully at his son, "I could have had more fun. But fun pretty much stops after university and marriage."

It had never occurred to Ron before that his father — and, come to think of it, his mother perhaps even more — might resent him simply for being able, sometimes, to enjoy life. When they were teenagers his mother's anxiety was such that she could not sleep until both boys came home. It was not love, it was neurotic anxiety, perhaps even hatred. But what a gloomy lot we are, he thought now. Not a fun-loving bunch. Well, right now there is finally something concrete, *death*, to be gloomy about.

At fifty-four, Ozzie was bald on the top of his head and had been, until his operation, somewhat overweight. But now he was wasted-looking. He rocked himself slowly back and forth all day. There was usually a cooling breeze. His wife came out with a tray only at lunchtime. She no longer fussed over him as she had before the operation. Now they largely ignored one another, except that she would fetch beer for him. He could still get to the bathroom by himself. They had avoided each other for years. It was much too late to change the pattern. It would perhaps have even been inconsiderate and insensitive to do so.

Ron felt he could read his mother's mind too. A kind of shorthand message emanated from her silence. A woman gets married, and has children and raises them. What else is she to do? The children go away, the man goes away inside himself, what is left for her? Now he is dying, but no more urgently than he plodded through all the dull years of living.

What did people do with "adult" life? Inured to the drab spectacle of his parents' existence for so long, Ron now began to be depressed by it. He felt *grief* — not so much for his father's approaching death as for all the years he and they had lived, and learned to live or at least exist, in this claustrophobic atmosphere. No wonder university had been such a relief.

He now slept again in the front room that he and Mike had shared as children. He automatically chose the top of the bunkbed. Mike, though older, had always fallen out of the top. Ron never did. When he couldn't sleep he looked from the end of the bed through the window at the street below just as he had done as a child. He heard the roaring of the waters striking rock.

The Indians, he remembered, half asleep, were careful to keep on the good side of the thunder-god. But we haven't done that. And so the place is cursed, he fantasized. He had recently read a book about the Indian tribe called by historians the "Neutrals", who had lived in the area before the Europeans came looking to make a profit of whatever they could find. Well, it was too late now to know what it might have been like here before there were twin American and Canadian cities. And highways and motels and honeymooners and wax museums and hydro and chemical plants. And "the cut". The "unkindest cut", he thought. But back then there were just the forest and the waterfalls and the cliffs and the river. . . .

"I went to work at the age of fifteen," said Ozzie. "I had to. My father's latest business venture had just gone bankrupt. There were four of us then — one in the States now" — I know, thought Ron — "and one girl in Montreal. Married a Catholic pea-souper, so my mother never forgave her. I didn't think it mattered so much myself who she married. Mother didn't like her marrying at all, I don't think. Where was I? Oh, yes. I went to work over the river in a warehouse. Moving things in and out mostly. Furniture. Very boring. But I made some wonderful pals. They're good mixers, Americans, better than we are. I never knew what happened to that gang afterwards though. Most went in the war, I suppose. Probably some dead. But that was years and years later, of course. Come to think of it, some of them would be fairly old by then; most were older than me, so maybe they didn't go to war. This was even before the Depression, when you could still get a job. I worked for five years at that warehouse. Then I got a job with the Company. My father had once worked for them. They thought I was quick, so they paid my way to university. By then there were no jobs, so I was lucky."

Lucky.

Ron found it difficult to think of Ozzie as young or "quick". He had retired permanently to bed now. One morning he simply didn't get up, didn't get dressed and go out to the rocker on the porch. It was August. Now Ron popped in to see him when he got home from work. They had moved the television set in so that Ozzie could watch baseball games; usually he fell asleep in the middle.

Mike came over every few days. Ron could see that Mike realized that to drop in every day would seem unnatural and would only annoy the old man. Only if he were living there, as he wished he could during this period, would he be expected each day, as Ron was expected. It was ironic. If he had known his father was going to die this summer, Ron would probably have wanted to travel in the opposite direction. Young Ron did not think he loved his father, though he felt a new interest in him and compassion for him now. It was Mike who should be in attendance, but who could not be because his nervous wife Lois (who was, Ron saw, basically the same sort of woman as their mother) was carrying his child in another house.

At least he's got that new life, Ron thought. At this moment I have only them, the parents I should love but probably haven't for God knows how long, and his dying, and her different kind of death. Look at yourself. Estranged inside from your whole family. Without caring. Much. Without even any drama or serious quarreling. Such deadness. Is the trouble with me or with them? Or both? Well, at least I'm here for the summer, doing what I can. Then away again, thank God. But Ron felt guilty in some vague, general way, guilty that he wasn't more upset than he was, or that he didn't feel *more* guilty.

His job was a farce. If only Mike knew how true his taunts were. The Customs Department did its bit for higher education by hiring far more university students than they needed except at the busiest moments of the tourist season. Most of the time there was very little to do; Ron read a lot of novels. When he was required to inspect an American tourist's car — glove compartment, front and back seats, the trunk — he hoped he would find nothing suspicious; he didn't know how he would deal with it if he caught someone smuggling, an activity commonplace in the area for as long as he could remember. He half closed his eyes when looking.

Soon Ozzie grew too weak to talk very much. The largely uneventful story of his life subsided. He slept a lot; Dr. Palmer had come to give him stronger pain-killers.

"I don't think he's going to last much longer," said Harriet one evening.

"No, I guess not," Ron said. "What will you do?"

"I can't think about it now. I'm prepared to deal with the death. But I can't make myself think what I'll do afterwards. Perhaps visit my cousin Alice. We were once very close."

Harriet's father was still alive in a nursing-home somewhere at the age of eighty-something, but she would not visit him, he knew. Young Ron had never met his surviving grandfather and probably never would.

"And you," she said, "what are you going to do? After you graduate next year."

"I thought I might travel in Europe for a year. And then maybe do graduate work."

"Do you really want to do graduate work?"

"Probably not," Ron answered, surprising himself.

"Nobody wants to work at all any more, it seems," observed his mother. "But you'll have to do something, to live."

Harriet now slept in the back corner room that had once been Ron's. Ozzie lived in the double bed in the master bedroom.

Ron was up front overlooking the street.

Ozzie died early in September 1960, quite silently (as far as they could tell) in the middle of the night. He looked just as stolid as usual.

Two days later there was a service followed by burial at the cemetery — where Old Queen Harold, young Ron remembered, was supposed to have taken his boys at midnight years ago to give them blow-jobs. Was that true? Was he still at it? It struck Ron that this was all he had ever known about the cemetery: he had never been in it before. The ceremony seemed quite unreal to him, so that irrelevant thoughts about old Harold wandered into his head. He wanted suddenly to giggle, as if he were still fourteen years old.

(*Lisan, where are you? I loved you.*)

Mike was dressed in a suit for the first time in years, and Ron's mother wore a black dress and veil. Pregnant Lois also wore a black dress. The minister whom Ozzie had disliked was speaking words that were lost almost immediately in the initially light but steadily gathering wind. It was, appropriately, Ron supposed, a dull gray day.

Steve was there, though Ron hadn't yet had a chance to speak to him. He hadn't seen him in a long time. And Steve's father, whose wife had died the year before. Ron

hadn't attended that funeral, though he had liked Steve's
mother — he'd been at university and hadn't wanted to
come home for it — and now he felt guilty.

His father, that defeated man, was dead. There was
nothing now except his faded and, behind her veil, half-
invisible mother, and, yes, her long-discarded and impla-
cable old father, between Ronald Benson and death. The
invisible. . . .

The coffin is lowered into the grave.

The earth is heaped upon the wooden coffin. A dark
sky presses down from above, but offers nothing of water
to the dry, windy ceremony. Earth, dark air. Gravestones
and scattered trees. Nothing of water. Certainly nothing of
fire. If you close your eyes, this is all unreal, Ron thought. If
you close your eyes even a little against the stinging wind,
the world dissolves, resolves itself into semblances, vague
shapes and shadows of amorphous night. . . .

Afterwards friends and neighbors came to the house for
sandwiches and cakes and sherry. The neighbor women
had managed most of this. Steve came with his father but
without his wife. Steve came more on Mike's account than
on his own, Ron saw. He and Mike had become friends
working together at the Company. There now seemed no
difference in their ages. But Steve was friendly to Ron too.

"I guess you must know a hell of a lot by now," he said
good-naturedly.

"Nothing useful," Ron replied.

And then at that moment he had a strange sensation. He
seemed all at once to be floating somewhere over this small
gathering, looking down on them, on himself along with
the rest. On young Ron talking with a piece of cake on a
paper napkin in one hand and a small glass of sherry in the

other. Am I drunk? he thought. He hadn't eaten that day. Or had he now *become* his father?

It was a moment only.

A few days later, on his day off, Ron was looking for an old diary he had once kept. He wanted to take it to Toronto. He seemed to remember hiding it in the attic. So he went up the stairs from his old back room into the cramped space under the v-shaped low roof. He had come here as a child to escape from the others.

It was dark, but he found a book in the corner by the top of the stairs where he had once stored his treasures. Only it wasn't, he discovered when he had come down again, his own diary. It was an old diary of his father's. Left there for him to find? Impossible. It must have been among those things simply shoved upstairs when they moved in. It must have been kept in the nineteen-thirties. When he was young, it seems, Ozzie had needed to say things in writing just as he had needed to speak certain things in the summer of his dying.

Most of it, he found, was quite ordinary. Brief records of dances, tennis, canoeing to Centre Island, playing bridge, attending varsity football games. Why had Ozzie bothered to record these things? Was he afraid that they would otherwise be lost to memory? But Ron read on, for he knew Harriet must soon appear.

Ozzie and Harriet. Ozzie and Harriet went canoeing together often once he had met her at a late spring dance and determined to win her. They were, he learned to his surprise, an outdoorsy couple. Ozzie had approached her at the fateful dance because she was sitting dejectedly by herself in a corner and she "looked so unhappy". He had wanted to rescue her, then. She was dark and beautiful, he said.

There followed much canoeing, long walks, chaste pleasures of a chaste Depression courtship. Did he wear a straw boater? The diary specified little in the way of clothing. Did she wear a light summer dress and a sun hat? Somehow Ron saw them as Edwardians even though it was the "dirty thirties". Dancing. Going to the pictures. Actually stealing a kiss in Queen's Park on a warm summer's night.

There were less happy times. "Saw Harr. this afternoon for an hour. Very melancholy. Nothing I could say or do seemed to make a difference."

And on and on through dances and movies and secret meetings until finally Ozzie was introduced to Papa at tea. It did not go well. "Rev. Listowel seemed determined to dislike me." Ozzie now "determined" to marry Harriet. Was it partly because of the father's hostility? Papa had certainly set his face against it. This made it quite romantic, Ron thought. Still, the elopement was decidedly less dramatic than that of Elizabeth Barrett and Robert Browning under somewhat similar circumstances. Indeed, it was hardly an elopement at all. Harriet went to stay with her cousin Alice (who had never married, Ron now recalled) and then wrote to her father that she was going to marry Ozzie in a certain Lutheran church on a certain day. He was welcome to come if he wanted to. He did not.

"I wish I could be more certain that we are doing the right thing," wrote Ozzie on the day before his wedding. "It occurs to me now how little we really know each other. But I suppose that's always the case with young love."

The next day's entry was the last one: "The deed is done. At St. Paul's Church in Islington this afternoon.

Harr. lovely in her mother's white lace dress — like a lady of the last century. I was nervous and fumbled when Bob gave me the ring. The reception at Alice's went very well with speeches, etc. I am writing this in the hotel. Harr. is asleep now. Too tired for me to want to bother her now. There will be time for that. She is still shy with me and wouldn't let me see her undress. Soon now I will lie down beside her, careful not to disturb her sleep. I do hope it is all for the best. I had to marry some time as every man does. In any case, what's done is done."

Ron was lying on top of the bunk bed. He could hear his mother moving about below in the kitchen at the other end of the house. She had returned then from her first shopping expedition since the funeral.

He slid down off the bed with a thump. He put the diary in his suitcase, where several other books were already packed for the return to Toronto.

SEVEN

◆

The chemicals now seep through the porous limestone of the escarpment and on into the river. Flowing to the great cliff's edge. The polluted falls: tainted wonder of the world.

My father, dead these twenty-five years and more, was a chemical worker. Let me give, as bluntly and coldly as I can, the context for his death.

During and after the war, chemistry was a major industry just over the river. This area has had one hundred and seven dumps for chemical waste. There have been more chemical plants here than anywhere else in North America. That is how the misnamed Love Canal became polluted with dioxin, the most dangerously toxic chemical waste known.

A man on my street in Toronto once lived by the Love Canal. He remembers swimming in it as a boy, then developing boils the size of silver dollars. He has lymph cancer. Among those still living near the Love there have been birth defects, unexplained miscarriages, all kinds of cancers, as well as emphysema and other respiratory disorders.

The canal was filled in decades ago, but in recent times the chemicals have come up out of the ground, burning the feet of children and dogs. As if the very earth were angry at us.

Some people say there was even earlier dumping of atomic wastes from the Manhattan Project in the 1940s, but this has not been proven. They say there is a silo of radioactive wastes that is leaking. They say there is TNT and nerve gas buried near by. Such rumors are probably inevitable. It is my neighbor, a man slowly dying, who gathers these stories from newspapers, from television programs, and from old friends or relatives, and then, like some contemporary ancient mariner, seizes upon me — on the street, in the subway car while we travel downtown — to report them in his hoarse, thin voice of doom.

The havoc we inflict upon the world in the name of progress we inflict upon ourselves. Our lust for mastery has become a kind of suicide. As the chemicals flow over the cataract to taint our water supply. As the remnants from Chernobyl fall, joining the acid rain, from the once-innocent air. As the hole in the ozone layer grows and grows.

My father's death was perhaps a small event in this continuing large context — part of the fruits of industrialism. He worked in chemicals. More than that, his research in Memphis and Joplin contributed, distantly, or so I was always told, to the Manhattan Project. Later he joined the New York chemical complex. In a sense he joined America.

America has been the industrial center, the world's nerve-center, quite inevitably — as if all the frenetic energy of mass production here has been only a speeded-up extension, a speeded-up film, if you like, of the ancient native energies of this dream-continent, this dynamo, contained in microcosm in the waterfall itself. There may be a tragic inevitability here: power breeds power to the point of self-destruction. Our civilization is perhaps not merely a machine (as it has so often been depicted) but also a natural force, even an organic growth that is quite out of control. Cancerous. Gone insane. Intoxicated with speed. In a word: *toxic*. (Ironically, the Neutrals were the first to grow tobacco in this area: a natural poison whose malignancy our civilization has greatly enhanced.)

My father has been dead a long time. But as I grow toward my own death, the age accelerates. "Ours is essentially a tragic age," D.H. Lawrence wrote of the aftermath of the First World War, "so we refuse to take it tragically." I would like to refuse myself. But after all this time, events conspire to make my father's face rise up before me: an image of man bewildered and destroyed by larger process. Though he was not of any special importance to the world. He was only one individual caught up in the age. Only one of its victims. A single chemical worker among many. A part that was dispensable, replaceable.

My father was a creature of the Company, of the culture of industrial growth, i.e., of cancer. I believe the Company provided him not only with his living but also with his death. Perhaps it functioned as his true God.

It was the Company, of course, that provided sickness and then death benefits.

EIGHT

◆

The following spring Ron graduated. He went to work as a customs officer for another summer in order to save money. His plans were still indefinite. But he intended to spend a year in Europe before doing any further study.

I now found that my mother's daily life had greatly changed. She went out a lot — something unheard-of before. She had "activities".

She had joined a bridge club. She and Ozzie had not played bridge in years. There was also the ladies' travel club — only a few of whose twenty or so members had ever ventured far outside of darkest Ontario. Then there was, more significantly as it turned out, a group of men and women that met each month in the public library to discuss "great books" under the general supervision of one of my former high school teachers. Harriet had taken to reading again for the first time since her marriage. She no longer watched television very much.

To young Ron's surprise, and to his unexpected chagrin,

she demanded relatively little of his time and attention. Or Mike's, for that matter. Ron had thought he would have to fend off a lonely middle-aged mother's typical expectations and demands this summer. But she asked very little.

Her new activities were, I suppose, commonplace. But she herself was mysterious to me now. I felt I did not know her any more. I wanted to know her better, talk with her, before I left home forever.

I thought that perhaps this new Harriet was the woman I had known as a child. Someone powerful, mysterious. Before she dwindled into fussiness and nervousness.

She was not fussy now. She was silent. She no longer felt the need to break the silence of the old house with speech, any speech. Now it was, ironically, I who needed to do that. I wanted to speak of the family before it dissolved altogether. But she knew no such imperative, it seemed. "If I told you, you wouldn't believe me anyway" — this was her unspoken message. She no longer interrogated me, as she had done once, about my plans and activities. I was on my own.

We ate meals together in a loud silence, punctuated only by my disjointed remarks about the minor happenings of the job, the day, and by her offhand, polite responses. We were like marionettes in a puppet play of domesticity. I was a little shocked to realize that I had always depended upon her attention and taken it for granted.

One evening we were both at home — a rare thing. I was determined to edge her into serious conversation.

"You're keeping busy," I observed.

"I've always been busy," Harriet said, guardedly.

"But you go out more now."

"I have more time that is my own, that's true."

We were sitting in the living-room. Harriet was dressed more smartly than ever before, at least in my memory, in a matching gray skirt and blouse. Her partly gray, partly black hair was more severely and neatly arranged than before. She had also lost some weight. Ron realized with a sudden surprise that she was not at all bad-looking for her age. This was a bit of a shock.

"You're looking very well."

"Thank you. I think I've been a little more 'health-conscious' this last year because of your poor father. My own father believed in regular exercise. And he's still alive. But your father never got enough exercise."

"That's not what killed him," I said bluntly.

"No."

"I'm sorry. I shouldn't have said that."

"It's only the truth, I'm afraid. Overweight didn't kill him, though he *was* overweight. It didn't kill him that he had so very few interests. But it didn't help him to live either."

I sat up in my chair. Harriet was seated in her own favorite chair with her legs elegantly crossed. I felt again that I didn't know her.

"Michael is very much like his father," she said then. It was as if she had recognized now that I wanted to talk about the family, and was willing to make this much effort to accommodate me. Even if she herself had thought the subject through and then put it aside. "You are more like me, I think."

"In what ways?"

"You want to better yourself. You've gravitated to Toronto, where I came from. You're not so fond of this town. I never have been either."

"But you don't leave."

"I can't afford to now. And my one grandchild is here."

Mike and Lois had a little girl. Harriet usually visited them on Sundays.

"We were going," continued Harriet, "to find a small place in the suburbs. But then came your father's illness."

"I didn't know that," I said.

"We were one of those couples," said Harriet, "who discovered as the years passed that we didn't really have all that much in common. But you try to accommodate each other in marriage."

"Do you wish you had married someone else?" I could scarcely believe that I was asking this question, or that she might answer it. But I might never have another chance.

"I don't know. There wasn't anybody else. My father scared anybody else off."

"He was a hard man?"

"He identified with God." She looked thoughtful. "Yes, that's it. He had the terrible need, the *insecurity* of God. For confirmation. Oh yes. . . . And for dominance too."

I was astonished. I had never in my life heard my mother speak like this. She was probably surprised at herself.

"God is very hungry," she said then quietly.

I stared at her. Her expression was just as cool and composed as before.

"I don't understand."

"*His* God was very hungry," she said. "A 'jealous God'. Perhaps there is another, I don't know."

"Yes," I said. "I understand now. Weren't you sorry for him?"

"Sorry for God? Well. Perhaps I should have been. I was too desperate then. To escape. After I married he wouldn't speak to me."

"Maybe he would now."

"It's too late, I think."

So she had defeated the God of her childhood. She had

defeated her husband too. My father. What might she not do to me?

"You won't stay here," said Harriet, as if reading my thoughts. "I would never try to keep you. Not after what was done to me."

I had never, of course, intended to stay. But now I felt more alone than I had ever done in my life.

Alone. Still, nothing stays the same for long in this world of "sick transit". Everything is always changing. Even in this moribund but roaring vale of tears. This city. . . .

Soon Steve and his wife Annie had their old friend Ron to dinner. He was pleased, of course, to see them. Annie was a pleasant and solid enough girl, he had always thought, if without any great conversational staples outside of her domestic life. Unfortunately, she had also invited a friend, a somewhat insipid typist whom Ron remembered vaguely from Grade Nine. He steeled himself to be "nice" to the girl and to see her home afterwards.

Steve and Annie's two kids, a boy and a girl, were cranky and quarrelsome this evening. They complained and whined their way through dinner. This made adult conversation more or less impossible.

Till Laurie, Annie's friend, who had turned out to be prettier and nicer than Ron expected, assisted her in getting the children to bed. She thought they were "cute". Ron did not. He volunteered to help Steve do the dishes. And they were friendly enough but soon found that they had little to say to one another there in the kitchen.

"Did you know," asked Steve, after some inconsequential chat, "that that old flame of yours was in town again? I didn't want to mention it in front of the girls."

"Old flame?" He had no idea at this moment what Steve meant.

"Yeah. I can't remember her name, it was something funny. Good-looking dark girl, the one we met in Buffalo that time. Her brother was in the Mafia or something. Well, she's working at the tourist bureau again. Barry saw her."

She was not with Carl. Steve had said earlier in the summer that Carl's parents had told him that, once again, Carl would not make it back from California at all this summer. His parents had seemed a little hurt and puzzled about this.

But Lisan was back — after three years. Why?

She was an illusion, he had long ago decided. A creature and reflection of frenetic America, not real. But he wanted to see her again, he thought out of sheer curiosity. What had she become? Was she more settled at all? He could look at her, perhaps talk with her, and then go off (or back?) to Europe and forget her forever.

In another mood he wanted to fuck her in cold blood, *use* her brutally though not violently, and then just leave her. She had it coming. He was surprised at the anger that surfaced in him during these fantasies. "Get your balls back," as Carl had said once to Steve when Annie, then his steady girlfriend, had briefly decided that she wanted to go out with someone else. His anger aroused him sexually. But "fantasy", on a Sunday afternoon when his mother was out, could only do so much for him.

Still, he waited for two weeks before going down to the falls to find her.

She did not look any older. But she seemed more vulnerable.

"I wondered if you were in town," she said evenly.

"Then why didn't you phone me?"

"I thought maybe you hated me."

"All that was three years ago," said Ron in as tough and neutral a voice as he could summon. "This is now. What are you doing back here?"

"Maybe I wanted to find you."

He shrugged this aside, as not worth serious consideration. He was determined to be hard with her. The very sight of her, still young, dark, and lovely, both irritated and aroused him.

"What are you doing at lunch–time?"

"Nothing," she said simply.

"My house is empty. My mother's out at a 'luncheon' meeting of her *fucking* travel club."

So we went, by taxi, back to the house. I didn't care if the neighbors noticed or not. I could always tell my mother that I had invited a friend to lunch.

We went up to my old back room, now unused. I closed the twenty-year-old venetian blinds. We took off our clothes without speaking.

I wanted to punish her.

This was the most exciting sex Ron had yet had. This was to be the summer of his vindication. He enjoyed being master.

For Lisan too had changed. She now seemed oddly submissive, even eager to please. She was more demanding, though, than she had been three years before. Her precious independence seemed to have worn thin. There was a new, or at least a more obvious, vulnerability about

her. She drank more — but she was never exactly drunk.
She had a dingy one-room apartment on a rundown street
downtown. Some nights I slept most of the night with her
there. But I always left her and went home before morning.
I wanted her to feel that I could do without her.

Some Sundays we went to the beach. But we never
made love there now.

She told me, of course, about Carl, or as much as she
knew. She had left him when he got too serious about her.
She wanted to look around, and did. She got a little but not
a lot of modelling work, and hoped to do some acting. But
attractive and talented girls were a "dime a dozen" there,
and it was discouraging. She began to feel inadequate and
insecure. Carl would turn up every once in a while, till
finally she got her current lover to throw him out of her
apartment one night because he was so drunk and obstreperous. Later she heard that he had dropped out of Berkeley and was moving with a fast crowd who were into
various kinds of drugs. Both uppers and downers. Drugs
were common in California, she said. She had even taken
some herself.

I wondered if Carl's parents knew that he had dropped
out of university. I thought that they were still sending him
money.

Lisan had found the pace too fast for her in California.
"I wasn't sure just who I was any more," she said. She had
wanted to be someplace quiet for a while. She said that she
had always thought of me as relaxing. She said the falls
relaxed her too, carried her out of herself when she looked
at them.

"I thought you were tough beyond your years," I said. I
was being deliberately sarcastic.

"So did I. And I was, I suppose. But now . . . Oh, I suppose I could be tough again if I *had* to be. But it's tiring being tough all the time, it wears you down. Maybe you'll find that yourself."

Ron found it rather exhilarating being tough. He almost thought he knew how the hoods of the Centre gang felt. He who had — after childhood with his brother — never been in a physical fight in his life.

"Poor Carl," said Lisan. "He wasn't up to life there either."

"So now you want peace and quiet. You're becoming a Canadian."

"Maybe I am," she said.

She was still intelligent, observant. In her own way she was quite shrewd.

But she was frightened now, too, she needed frequent reassurance. She wanted to make love almost constantly, it seemed. Something had made her a little desperate, and young "tough" Ron was quite willing to take advantage of it. But it also exhausted him at times.

I have trouble remembering the exact order of things. That long, hot summer. . . .

I know I seldom took her anywhere except the beach. We were both saving money. She would often cook small meals in her room.

I wasn't yet able to forgive her. I still wanted to hurt her.

So I said, one evening, casually:

"Well. What's next for you? After this *interlude.*"

"Who knows?" she said, stung a little. "And you?"

"Europe. I'm going to meet someone there. Later, graduate school, I guess."

"Graduate school."

She was wearing a cheap white bathrobe. She had just washed her lovely dark hair in the bathroom down the hall.

"Hold me," she said then. "Make love to me."

I did, but then I left right away. I could still smell her damp hair as I walked home.

"I have to go now," I said. "I'll see you tomorrow, maybe."

This is perhaps not quite exact factually. It is a typical episode. The *sort* of thing that happened. As I sift and sift the shifting memory of that summer through my mind.

I haven't yet told the whole truth. Sure, I wanted to punish her. But I was still afraid of her too.

She did strange things. And then I found myself doing strange things. As if I was catching her like a disease.

She had phobias now. She wouldn't go out of her apartment alone at night. I had to come over if she wanted to go to the corner store for milk. She *saw* things, she said, in the dark part of people's lawns. Then I began to notice strange things myself. But they were nothing, of course, when investigated.

A cat crossing the night street could upset her.

And this was the same girl who had once seemed so self-sufficient and fearless.

She had nightmares sometimes, though she refused to describe them. She only wanted to make love again when I woke her. So I began to dream strange dreams too. At home in my own bed.

I dreamed that we were in that bedroom in Buffalo. The large hairy man lay on the bed, his throat cut. But this time he was still alive, he was making loud rasping sounds, attempting vainly to speak. . . .

I dreamed we were once again at the police station being questioned. Exhausted, guilty. Only this time the officer had found my penknife in my jacket pocket. It was all bloody. "Why did you do it?" he repeated. Over and over. "Why did you do it? It'll be better for you if you admit everything now." He was a menacing seven-foot Negro with a huge beer-gut.

Another time I dreamed of California. I saw Carl and Lisan making love on a deserted beach inlet. Their naked bodies were all golden. They were dusted with fine sand. They were completely beautiful. But the tide was coming in, though they didn't care, the rising tide was coming in to drown them. . . .

I would wake up in a cold sweat.

But outwardly, with Lisan, I tried to maintain my "cool" demeanor. I wouldn't let her know she had so much effect on me. That could only lead, surely, to disaster.

She did strange things. She would stand at her window for half an hour, looking out at nothing, apparently seeing nothing, refusing to speak to or answer me.

At home, on the top of the bunk bed once again, I looked out on chaos, night's writhing lines and streaks. Till, as in my childhood, I fell asleep there.

If only we had reached out more. Each of us. But we were frozen, it seemed, in a pattern of intransigent youth.

It soon seemed that she wanted me for a purpose. For one day she said:

"Do you want to go to Buffalo with me?"

"Not much. Do you have to go?"

"Yes. I want to see my parents. If they'll see me."

"Why?"

"They're still my parents."

"Yes." He felt the same, of course. And he found, to his surprise, that he was sorry for her.

"You don't want to go with me," she said.

"No. But I will." Has this happened before, he wondered. He sensed some echo in her words.

"Thank you. I need some support there. Just for the day."

So they drove over on a Saturday in a rented car. It was years since Ron had been in Buffalo, and years since Lisan had seen her parents. But she did not phone ahead. She was afraid they would refuse to see her if she gave them any warning. So they took their chances.

"What if they're out all day? Or away?"

"Then that's fate."

Ron drove. Lisan was very tense. She smiled only once en route.

"They'll think you're Italian," she said. "You're dark enough."

"They're not *both* Italian, are they?" He thought he remembered this from the first night they had met.

"Just my mother. My father is English and Scottish in background."

"Just like me," said Ron.

"The Church insisted that we be raised as Catholics. But I know that they used birth control. Or there'd have been more of us."

Us. Lisan and Angelo. Angelo. A fallen angel? A demon? Angelo Mason. He remembered the surname now from the newspapers. It was strange to have forgotten the last name of a girl you were sleeping with. But Lisan had never used it with him and she did not use it now. She was Lisan, period. Formerly Felicia. Felicia and Angelo. Felicia Elizabeth-Anne Mason? Quite a fancy name for a some-

time or would-be model and actress. She should have used
it all.

"The murder must have been devastating for them," he
ventured.

She did not reply.

He was thinking how little he knew about her, her
family, her background. Her whole social identity.

"You know, I've never seen Buffalo by day. It's not so
bad. It was always a city of night for us. Of darkness. . . ."

They had parked the car and gotten out. It was an
imposing brownstone house. There was a large front lawn,
neatly if somewhat antiseptically landscaped with small
junipers and a fir hedge. A two-car garage. No dogs or cats
in sight. A large picture window through which, no
doubt, Lisan and Ron could be seen drifting like ghosts of
the family past or future up the long front walk. What
alarmed eyes were touching them? He could sense them
there behind the glass, looking.

Ron banged the large brass knocker against the solid
oak door.

There was no response.

After a few moments Lisan pushed the bell. She still
looked frightened but determined. Through the narrow
vertical windows of the door a dark hallway could be seen.

Lisan pushed the bell again.

A light went on in the dark hallway.

A thin, middle-aged woman in an expensive beige suit
opened the door.

"Yes?" she said, slightly unpleasantly. She looked as if
she wondered what on earth this young pair was doing on
her doorstep.

Lisan was shivering, though the day was very warm.

"Mrs. Mason?" began Ron. He was conscious of Lisan's extreme discomfort.

"Mrs. *Mason?*" repeated the thin woman incredulously.

"Gone," said Lisan.

"Gone these four years," said the woman in the beige suit tartly. "Gone to Switzerland, I believe."

"Oh. . ." said Lisan helplessly.

"Her mother," explained Ron. "Her parents, that is. She hasn't seen them in years."

The woman's cool expression changed a little.

"I see. And you once lived here."

Lisan nodded. "Yes," she said.

"You'd better come in for a minute, then," said the beige woman with somewhat prim kindness. "I'll have the maid make us some tea. Though goodness knows where the creature has gotten herself to. She should have answered the door."

"You're very kind," said Ron, sounding (he thought) like his mother.

They followed the beige woman into a long, well-furnished living-room. Lisan sank into a leather chair as the woman disappeared out the far end.

"Don't faint," said Ron.

"No. I'll be all right. I just need to catch my breath."

"They left because of the scandal."

"Of course. Why didn't I know? I was so stupid. Of course that's what they'd do. They hated any kind of trouble. I must have been counting on them more than I admitted to myself."

In came a black, uniformed maid with a silver tea-service and some cups on a silver tray. This is unreal, Ron thought.

"Beryl," said Lisan in a low voice. But the woman

hurried away as though she had not heard. She had not looked at them.

Lisan was upset again.

"She was *our* maid. She knew me. She must have seen us through the front window and was afraid to answer the door. She used to be terrified of Angelo."

Presently the lady of the house returned.

"I am Evelyn Baxter," she announced. "My husband bought the house from your father. I'm afraid he got it for less than it was worth because of the circumstances. Here, let me give you some tea. I'm afraid I haven't any cakes or biscuits." She sat down at the table and began to pour. She passed a cup to Lisan and another to Ron. Her manner was brisk but not unkind. She spoke clearly and brightly as if playing a part on a stage.

"You're very kind," said Lisan, who had collected herself somewhat. "It never occurred to me that they would leave, though it should have."

"I didn't meet them, I'm afraid. My husband knew your father."

"I spent my childhood and most of my adolescence here," said Lisan. "When I wasn't away at school."

"I'll show you around," said Mrs. Baxter, though without much enthusiasm.

"No. I've imposed enough already. If I could just have a last look at the grounds out back."

After they had finished their tea they all went out through the kitchen into the large back garden. There was no sign of Beryl the maid.

"This is where my older brother used to play with me," said Lisan.

"We've had it redone, I'm afraid," said Mrs. Baxter.

You can't go home again.

They looked for what seemed a long moment. There

was a large expanse of lawn, neatly landscaped. Too neat, he thought.

And then Ron *saw* the child Felicia running from a huge, hairy man-ape. All the way down the long backyard. She was shrieking with childish, pleasurable fright. She wore a short white dress that showed her bare legs and knees. He wore black trousers and an unbuttoned black shirt. Like a Nazi. It was Beauty and the Beast. Till they disappeared behind the clump of trees at the bottom of the garden. Though possibly the small "grove" wasn't even there then, Ron thought.

"We must really be going," said the convent-trained young lady beside him. "You've been very kind to put up with this intrusion."

He came back to the day, the house, the expensive beige-clad lady. Lisan.

No doubt Mrs. Baxter would say to her husband later: "The most unexpected thing happened this afternoon. . . ."

"Not at all," she said now. "I'm only sorry I don't have your parents' address."

"I don't think," said Lisan, smiling ruefully, "that our reunion was meant to be. I have my own life now," she lied.

She was cast-off now, a castaway.

She was speaking rather quickly without, apparently, expecting a response.

"I thought I had a very happy childhood. My parents and my brother loved me. My brother spent a lot of time amusing me before he left home. He also got into a lot of trouble, but that didn't really register on me at the time.

"My childhood was *too* sheltered, I guess. I made up for that later on.

"I was the kind of spoiled rich girl who longs, romantically, to be poor, adventurous, free. Eventually, I got my wish. . . ."

The day had turned cloudy. It would rain soon — a cleansing summer shower. Ron concentrated on his driving.

Lisan suggested quietly, some days later, that perhaps it was time for her to go to Europe too. Ron said he wanted to go alone.

"We could go *over* together," she said. "On the boat." She had an idea she might find her parents in Switzerland.

"No," he said.

Soon he must leave her, he thought. But not just yet.

Don't you realize that you're in love with her again? he asked himself one day.

No. Surely he wasn't. She was too pathetic now, not the strong, mysterious girl he thought he had known. Yet he wanted to go on seeing her. For now. He was sorry for her, he told himself.

Meanwhile Lisan grew ever more strange, thin, nervous.

"Shouldn't I meet this girl you're seeing?"

"I don't think it will outlast the summer," I said. "I'm going away in the fall."

"Nevertheless," said Harriet. "You spend all your time with her."

"All right. I'll bring her over."

Harriet was not fond of Americans. She had disliked

Joplin and Memphis during the war years. And she thoroughly disapproved of Catholicism; in this she was still her father's daughter. She was not inclined, once she saw her, to give Lisan the benefit of the doubt.

We sat in our living-room and had tea. It was bizarrely reminiscent, I thought, of the recent scene in Buffalo, even though this was a much less expensively furnished room. My mother was being pleasantly vague with this strange young woman, but I felt that she might well speak her mind before the afternoon was over. I had recently learned to respect her new frankness. And I knew that she disliked most of what I had told her (omitting, of course, all reference to Angelo) of Lisan's life and background.

"You've been a model," said Harriet.

"Yes. But only for brief periods."

"You're very pretty. In an American way."

"Thank you."

"During the war, when we lived in the States, I knew several girls with your style of looks."

"I learned from modeling," said Lisan evenly, "that my type was nothing very special."

"You're very pretty, nevertheless. Don't you find Canada too staid for you?"

"No."

"Americans are usually so adventurous. Are you adventurous?"

Oh boy, I thought.

"I read something about Ernest Hemingway," continued Harriet, "in *LIFE* magazine. I think he says that he needs to live near the edge, close to death. Now, *that* is American, isn't it?"

I could sense now that Lisan was upset.

"I like to think I've outgrown that sort of compulsion," she said calmly.

"I think Mr. Hemingway contends that absolute freedom always involves being close to death," said Harriet. "Once I wouldn't have known what he meant."

"I'm not sure I know what freedom is any more," said Lisan. "Though I once went looking for it."

"So did I," said Harriet, "when I was young. I ran away from home too, you know." She paused, sipping her tea. "But I didn't get freedom then. Not until there was a death. It takes a death of some sort to be free. You'll discover that, if you haven't already."

Like a sibyl as she said this, she looked into her drained teacup. Then she set it down decisively.

Afterwards Ron and Lisan made love in her room. Tenderly, slowly.

Later, as she slept lightly in his arms, he began to think that he ought to take her to Europe with him. At least help her to find her parents. Then they would go their separate ways.

NINE

◆

A bright pink apartment building high against the blue
sky. Semi-circular balconies that jutted out over the steep
street. It was four stories, on Jackson near Mason, facing
north. The building seemed to float on the blue sky. Like a
ship, as he looked up at it. Small white clouds moved
behind it. It was warm in the autumn sunshine.

He went in.

There was an antique cage-lift with a sign that said
"Out of order". It looked very flimsy and dilapidated, in
any case. So he climbed laboriously up the stairs to the
third floor.

It was dark in the dingy hallway. Having come in from
the bright day, he could not see very well at first. It was
Apartment Five he wanted.

The door was dirty and needed painting. The old green
paint was chipped and cracked. He stood there for a
moment, almost afraid to knock. There was no sound
from within. Only the distant constant noise of the street,
like the surf in the bay. Then the rumble of a passing cable-
car. He thought, involuntarily, of the murmur of the falls:

at the white heart of life is the whisper of death.

He knocked.

It must have a north light, he thought, remembering the alcoves. It could be a painter's studio, perhaps had been in its time.

Someone was opening the door. A rather dirty-looking young blond man in jeans and a T-shirt. He needed a haircut and hadn't shaved recently. He was thin to the point of emaciation.

"Yeah, man?" His eyes were hollow, deeply shadowed. Like an unkempt Christ. Or someone in a concentration camp. Except the eyes now shifted nervously, rapidly.

"Don't you know me?"

"Should I?"

"Yes, dammit."

"Are you the connection?"

"No."

The man turned then and jerked back into the dark apartment, having simply lost interest, it seemed, in his visitor, who followed him into a living-room brightened at one end by the north light from the alcove window. He could see the bay and the island prison out there.

The unkempt young man was slouching now in an old, dirty-looking armchair. There was an equally old, collapsed sofa, and a dark, probably very dirty, rug. Nothing more, no tables or pictures, nothing.

Then he spoke quickly, jerkily.

"I was expecting him. Or her. Sometimes it's a her. There's nothing here but rotgut wine. In the fridge." And he waved in the general direction of another room. Then he laughed shortly.

"Do you really not know me?"

The man looked at him strangely then, as if to say what did it matter if he had known him all along, or known him once, sometime, somewhere, why did he think it mattered?

"I've gotta get some stuff," he said then.

"Carl, for Christ's sake. It's Ron. Ron Benson."

The surviving members of the Hill family had quickly located the body. They always knew where to look.

The police dealt with the matter as efficiently as usual. They were used to suicides at the falls. These were almost never reported or otherwise publicized. That would only encourage others, it was felt.

Ron told them what he knew. He showed them the letter, and they copied it for their files. They seemed quite satisfied that the young woman was mentally unbalanced and suicidal. Eyewitnesses made it clear that she had killed herself without immediate assistance from anyone else.

Lisan-Felicia Mason was cremated, at Ron's expense, and her ashes were scattered into the river from the Peace Bridge. Between two countries. He was the only witness and mourner.

He could not go to Europe yet. He had to go somewhere else first.

It was dusk outside now. They were well into the cheap red wine. Ron could not see Carl's face. There was no light in the living-room. But the wine seemed to make Carl a little more focused and lucid, for a while anyhow.

"I was at this outdoor bar," he said, "near Fisherman's Wharf. Having a beer. And this bearded cat sits down at my table. 'Why are you alone?' he said. He looked and sounded very drunk, or stoned. 'Why not?' I said. Then he shoved a couple of bills at me. 'Look,' he said, 'buy me a drink with this.' 'Buy yourself,' I said. 'I can't. They know

me here,' he said. So I said, 'That's between you and them.'
But then a waiter came and served him without any trouble. I began to think he was a bit nuts.

"He started to tell me next that he had to be very careful
because the Mafia was after him. What a nut-case, I
thought again.

"Then he spoke to a guy passing by our table. The guy
looked, then simply ignored him and went on.

"'Do you know him?' I asked.

"'I think he's a homosexual,' he said.

"'How can you tell?'

"'I have an eye for it. Don't you?'

"'No.'

"'Listen. You want to come to my place for a beer? It's
right near here.'

"Then I looked at him again because there was something about him. His voice too. And I said to him what you
said to me, 'Don't you know me?'"

"I have to find him," said Ron.

"He was my first connection."

Ron had had some trouble finding Carl. He had had to
pester two superintendents of apartment buildings to
search their untidy offices for a forwarding address. The
first had one conveniently at hand. The second promised
to find it, but said he might need a day or two — he was so
busy at present — before he could manage a search. Carl
had moved at least twice since the address still listed in the
phone book.

So Ron had spent a couple of days scrambling about the
city. And in spite of all the horror that had possessed him
and brought him here there was one ray of light: he liked
this place. Or he *would* like it if (or when) he could like any

place. It seemed to him a good place. A place of hope.

The people in his little old hotel on Taylor Street — the Hotel Mark Twain, as if this was perhaps where Huck Finn, escaping from corruption, had eventually fetched up — were relaxed and friendly. There was an easiness of social exchange that was rare back in Canada. Had he not been on an urgent mission he would have liked simply to relax here.

It was a city of light.

Carl was listed in the phone book but not immediately traceable. The number had been disconnected. Larry was not, of course, listed at all — at least, not under the name that he had been born with. That would have been too much to expect.

When the second of Carl's forwarding addresses proved empty, Ron realized that he might have to stay in San Francisco for some time before he made any progress. He had a limited amount of money.

Sometimes he walked up and down the steep hills. Sometimes he took the rumbling cable-cars. He liked the way people hung on to the sides of them. He went up Nob Hill through the steep pastel-colored streets (not knowing then how close he was to Carl's pink building), then down, and then up Russian Hill and down again to Fisherman's Wharf.

He went to Chinatown. He went to the central library and to the art museum. He took a bus west out Geary Street to the Cliff House on the edge of the ocean where the Seal Rocks and the frisking black seals could be seen. It was mild and sunny for several days. Perfect tourist weather.

On the fourth day he phoned the second superintendent to remind him of his promise. He had almost persuaded himself by now that he could not find Carl, that he ought just to relax and recover himself here in the city. A therapeutic stay. Let sleeping dogs lie: he would never, could never, forget Lisan or her story, but surely he could look ahead positively, not dwell on it obsessively. Not dwell on the dark side of things. It all seemed so far away from this bright city. Perhaps the super's ignorance or officiousness was a blessing after all. But he phoned, he had to phone.

To his surprise the busy man had kept his promise. He now had an address for him.

Jackson Street. By Nob Hill.

"She threw me out of her goddam apartment, you know."

"I know. She told me."

"I don't know why. She was on the stuff too, you know." He seemed resentful still.

"Carl, she's dead."

But Carl could not seem to take this in.

"I think Larry supplied her too. He had some hold over her, I didn't understand it. Every few months she'd have a different old man, but Larry was always still around. In the background."

"Do you think the Mafia was still after him?"

"Who knows? It was hard to think of him as a murderer." Carl laughed harshly.

"I loved her," he said then. "She had an excitement about her."

Then, his tone shifting rapidly again: "I can't pay my rent, you know. They're working themselves up to throw me out of here."

"I can't help you unless you go off drugs. You'll never have any money unless you do. You should come home and dry out. Your father's a doctor. He'll know what to do. And I *owe* him. But I can't help you unless you come back with me. I have little enough cash myself these days. I mean, I worked all summer but the money won't last that long."

"I can't go back," said Carl. And: "You were always so straight."

"How can you stay here?"

"Look. If I promise to go, will you lend me some money?"

"Not unless you come with me."

"You don't trust me."

"I don't know you, not like this. You were full of life and humor once. Back there."

Carl snorted derisively. Ron persisted:

"Have you eaten today? Come out to a restaurant. I'll buy you some supper." They had finished the wine. Ron was conscious now of being hungry.

"I've got an appointment," said Carl, slurring his words a little. "A very important appointment."

The room had an unpleasant, unidentifiable smell. His hunger made Ron more aware of it.

"Look. You don't have a phone. I'll go out and find a pay phone and order us a pizza."

Carl snorted once again.

"You do that. A pizza, for Christ's sake."

If I go, he'll look for his contact, Ron thought helplessly. The extent of Carl's deterioration was beginning to come home to him. He hadn't come to California very greatly worried about Carl, who had after all betrayed his friendship. But it was impossible here, now, in his presence, to remain unaffected.

"You need some food. Pizza, Chinese, whatever."

Carl's snarling smile was a kind of parody of his former

good cheer. He seemed now to be thinking about something.

"Tell you what," he said after a minute or so of silence. "I haven't seen old Larry in a long time. But there's a number somewhere in the bedroom. Let's look up old Larry. Tonight."

Ron saw where this was leading. For Carl. But what else could he do? He had to find Larry, in any case. He had to know.

Perhaps if I can get him out of here, get some food into him, we can proceed from there, he thought.

They descended the dark stairs. Carl's talk was quick, nervous, less coherent now. It was almost as if he had sobered up (or down) temporarily on the wine. Now he was high again.

"You won't recognize old Larry. Disguised in a beard. Got a scar on his cheek now. A large, long scar. I think maybe he did it to himself to change his appearance. Though maybe it was just that some cat didn't care for his 'advances' and cut him good." He laughed harshly at the thought.

They were walking down the dark, steep street. They came to a phone booth on a lighted corner.

"Give me some change," said Carl. "I might have to make several calls."

Another night and another day have passed. Ron is in a dimly lit bar on Geary Street. It is a dark room that might be anywhere in the world. Or any decade of the century. He is listening intently to his companion at a small corner table.

"Yeah, I gave him some last night. After you left. For old times' sake, if you like. He's got nothing now. His parents cut him off when they found out he'd quit school and wouldn't go home. I didn't want him going back there, blabbing about me. It might reach the wrong people. So I've supplied him cheap sometimes. When he was first really into it, I sometimes let him pay in kind. *If* you know what I mean. I see you don't. You always were very innocent. Hell, I mean with his body. He would do anything for it at that time. Still would, of course. But he's too wasted to be any good to me that way any more."

"How could you do it to him?"

"He just took to it. He couldn't function without it. Some people can handle it without getting that wasted. Lisan could. He couldn't. Look, it wasn't just me — he was getting it from several people. I couldn't have stopped him."

Larry was greatly changed in appearance. Bearded, graying prematurely. He looked older, more confident, cynical. The prominent scar had something to do with this. Ron did not know quite how to deal with him. He only knew that he must persist.

"I think you know what I want to talk about."

They were sitting in a small bar on Geary Street. They had a table to themselves, no one could hear their conversation. But still Larry seemed evasive, though he had agreed the previous evening to meet him here.

There had been a young black man at Larry's place the night before. He was named Lester. He did not seem to Ron to be a junkie or a criminal or a homosexual. Just a brash, jocular, friendly, and rather likeable guy. He seemed bright. He had gone to college for a while. He was now working as a bartender in a hotel. He talked a lot about the women he took to bed. He seemed to know Carl quite well. He seemed a good sort — he let Carl borrow five dollars. Ron had wondered if he could help him with Carl.

So he got his phone number. Lester left when it became clear that he would not be able to talk with Larry alone that evening. Carl insisted on staying.

"I've been into it myself pretty heavily at times," said Larry. "Quite blotto, in fact. But I've been able to cut myself off, too."

"I want to help Carl if I can," Ron said. "Take him home. But I didn't come here on his account. Do you know that Lisan is dead?"

Larry lit his cigarette. He had inserted it expertly into a long cigarette-holder. He wore gloves even indoors, a dark suit, a white shirt, and a dark tie. He wore glasses now too — he could have passed for a professor. Sometimes, he had told Ron already, he wore a cape — in cooler weather. He had a slightly British manner. A certain brittle quality. A front, Ron supposed. But then Larry was, as Ron had had to remind himself, not an American but a Canadian. Someone he had known in Grade One. Someone he and Carl, and Steve too, had played with in the field of long grass between the school and the Shredded Wheat factory. How had he become what he was now?

Larry had run away from home in his early teens and never come back. The story that went around at that time said that his older brother had caught him with "Old Queen Harold" in the cemetery and beaten him up. At the time Steve, Carl, and Ron, though shocked by the story, had felt guilty about always treating Larry rather badly. He had no father, said Steve, no wonder he was queer, he couldn't help it.

"I'm not at all surprised," Larry said smoothly. "Was it suicide?"

"How can you be so cool?" It occurred to Ron then that Carl might have told him about it the night before, that he was prepared.

"It was inevitable, my dear boy. She had a yen for the ultimate gesture. And she would never have wallowed in her miseries, or allowed people to pity her, as our truly pitiable Carl does.

"And" — he paused significantly — "she was guilty, of course."

On the phone that afternoon Lester was just as friendly as he had been the previous night. He allowed that he too had felt sorry for Carl. He agreed to have lunch the next day. Ron was to see Larry that evening.

The next day came. They met.

They lunched down by Fisherman's Wharf. Lester wore an open white shirt and a pair of dark–blue pants. He was a large, good-looking, smiling youth—confident, open. If he had ever suffered from American racism, Ron thought, he showed no sign of it now. For Lester life seemed to roll along pleasantly and easily.

"I'd like," said Ron, "to get him out of here and off drugs, if it's possible. That's the one thing that keeps me here now. After I talked things out with Larry last night."

"That Larry is really something," laughed Lester. "If he ever woke up beside a woman he'd likely die of shock. One night he was in the hotel bar where I used to work and he was really put out because there was no 'game' around. Just females. He was chatting one up to beat the band, but he wasn't very happy about it."

"He's a heroin dealer," said Ron shortly. He wanted to talk about Carl.

"A cat's gotta live," said Lester. "He was always a good tipper at the bar. And surprisingly successful with the foreign guys who were staying in the hotel. Which is why he came to that bar, I guess. I mean, cool, regular-looking guys. Tourists, you know. Especially Germans, for some reason. He was always saying to me, come round to his place for a drink. So I do, once in a while. He's always good for a drink on a dull evening when I'm not working and I don't have a honey lined up. I made it clear from the start that I'm not queer, of course. Hey, that rhymes."

Lester had knocked back his Scotch on the rocks in a few gulps. It made him talkative. Obviously he liked to drink if somebody else was paying. Booze was his thing, so he had probably not been tempted by Larry's other goodies. Ron ordered him another one.

"But what can we do about Carl? He's a friend of yours, isn't he?"

"I used to see him a lot a few years ago. He was okay then. I'd see him at parties. He was a lot of fun then. He had a groovy sports car, man, I guess he must have sold it to support his habit. We took out some of the same girls. Compared notes. Now he's wasted, man."

"He's an old friend of mine. I'd like to get him back to Canada."

"He won't go unless you kidnap him, believe me."

"I can't do that."

"He won't go freely. The way he is. You saw him."

"Yeah, I saw him," said Ron grimly.

"You appear to think I'm heartless," said Larry. "About Carl. And about Lisan, whom I always knew as Felicia back in Buffalo. She was one of my closest friends then. I'm not heartless, believe me, just hardened. So much happened. . . .

"Before I talk about Lisan I have to talk about myself. I've changed a lot. A shrink I had once said that homosexuals were like retarded children, whatever that was supposed to mean. Always regressing to childhood I guess is what he meant. And maybe there's some truth in that. But I've also grown much older in a very few years, a lot older than I really am. Times are changing, and I'm changing with them. I can't afford to indulge in too much sentiment, or I won't survive in this world. Most queers are sentimental and evasive — they live in their infantile fantasies. What the hell, everyone wants to go back to childhood, according to Freud. Only with some of us the urge is stronger, and takes peculiar forms.

"For instance, I'll tell you a story. When I first came here, on the run, I had already grown a beard. I didn't have the scar yet — that was the result of a little contretemps a year or so later. I had let my hair grow quite long so people would think I was some kind of artist or poet. A beatnik. They're indulged here, you know, thought of as harmless.

"One night I was in a bar, on the lookout, you might say, when a guy came in, about my age, a dark guy. He was a bell captain in a big hotel. He told me he had come from the Philippines a few years before. He got very chummy and said he was wild about my beard. He said he wanted to stroke it.

"Well, he invited me back to his place. We went to bed right away. And he continued to want to stroke my beard, off and on, all night long. In the morning, after we had made love a second time, we were lying there and he said, 'You know, I had a dream about you. I dreamt that I saw you in upstate New York and you were driving a pickup truck to your place in the country. Then I was with you, sitting beside you, and I knew that we were going to live there. . . .' I realized I had told him the night before — I know now that it was stupid to be so accurate — that I was from northern New York State.

"Then it was light, and I was awake again, though my

Filipino had gone back to sleep. On one wall over the bed, I saw now, was a huge crucifix. On the other was a large colored picture of Jesus looking down on us with the most tender expression in the world in his eyes. He had a soft, flowing brown beard. He looked very loving. It quite shook me up — even though I was never religious.

"I got up a bit hastily. My friend slept on. Obviously, he had been raised as a Catholic in the Philippines. I stumbled to the bathroom, and then I looked around the apartment, because I was curious about him. I was even more startled by what I saw then.

"On the walls of his living-room *and* his dining-room were huge blown-up photographs of very muscular naked men. Black, Asian, white. Rather amateur photography. I had never seen anything like it. Buffalo was never like this, I thought. I mean, people might keep photographs of that kind in a drawer. But not blown up on the walls. I thought, wow, this is California all right.

"I went back and looked at him again. He was small, though muscular, himself, nothing like as impressive as his pin-ups. He was still asleep, and he was now curled up in the fetal position. Under his religious icons.

"When I reached the street I realized what it was that alarmed me about this whole scene. What I couldn't handle at all.

"He thought that I was Jesus, you see. . . ."

Lester and Ron were riding up the hill on a crowded cable-car chock-full of San Franciscans and tourists. Lester sat on one of the outside wooden seats smiling broadly while Ron stood, leaning outward, holding on to the pole directly in front of his new friend. Thus their legs brushed against one another occasionally, which made Ron slightly embarrassed, though he hoped that this didn't show. Touch didn't embarrass Lester. Occasionally he reached his hand out to steady Ron, though he laughed as well when Ron lost his balance a little. Everything seemed funny to Lester, Ron thought. And there they were, part of a dream: a black man and a white man together in America.

City of light.

They were both a little high from their largely liquid lunch. Later, walking in the clean air and the warm sun, Ron could believe, almost, that good was still possible here. This place was surely the hope of America. Perhaps also the illusion. Or was this just Canadian suspiciousness, loyalist paranoia? The American dream: the quick, brief friendship of strangers. Even if it was an illusion, it was a good one. Even dwarfed by the steep streets. And now the large pink building loomed over them as well, like a birthday cake with its birthday promises.

"Angelo was a bastard. He deserved to die. He treated me like shit."

"Felicia said you enjoyed it."

Larry smiled thinly.

"Touché, my friend. Well, perhaps. Perhaps I did at one time. But I came to hate him too."

"Why was she guilty? You killed him, didn't you?"

"I don't think I should admit that, even to you."

"Well, whoever killed him: why was *she* guilty? She was with me that night."

"I remember that well. In spite of the condition I was in."

"Well. Why?" Ron persisted.

"She wanted him dead. She blamed him for all her problems. It seems he had molested her. I never knew, incidentally, whether I should believe that story or not. Angelo didn't like women at all, didn't like them anywhere near him."

"But she didn't kill him."

"She tried. She wanted him dead. She even wormed out of me the name of one of Angelo's more vicious 'rivals' in the organization. Then she approached him with a proposition. She would sleep with him if he would kill Angelo. *How* didn't matter."

"I don't believe that."

"It does seem far-fetched, I know. But she told me about it herself. I suppose it could have been one of her fantasies, though I believed it at the time. She was quite convincing, and angrier than ever. You see, the man reneged. He slept with her all right, but he didn't dare to kill Angelo — even though he hated him too. Everyone did, believe me. But he cheated her. At least, at that time."

Ron did not know whether to believe any of this or not. But Lisan was, by her own written account, crazy, was she not? Crazy, in a crazy world. Anything might be possible there.

"There's more," said Larry. "There's no reason to conceal the rest now. On the night you came and found me with Felicia she was not merely comforting me. She had been actively *urging* me to kill her brother. Until you came. I was in a terrible, desperate state, half out of my mind with speed, and she saw that I might do anything when I was like that. She was very clever, very shrewd, our Lisan. She knew how to play on people's weaknesses.

"So you see, when I phoned—because I thought that she should be the first to see what she had accomplished— knowing that she would come right over (with you, as events apparently fell out), she knew what she would find. Unless things had gone wrong. So you were useful, you see. As an innocent Canadian alibi. Possibly, as protection, though you'd have been no match for Angelo. . . ."

His voice trailed off.

"I don't believe it," said Ron.

"The oddest thing," Larry continued in his peculiarly bland voice, "is that she blocked it out for years. I mean, her participation in the death. She actually *forgot* that she had enlisted people. It was only when I found her in L.A. — she had left Carl (or was it the one after him? I forget) to do some modeling in L.A. But I found her out of work and offered her a place to stay if she would come back here. So she came. I wanted her where I could keep an eye on her."

"*And* keep her on speed."

Larry did not reply at first.

"She was a doomed child," he said. "I could at least have looked after her. I had *mastered* my weaknesses, my nature — learned to *control* them. But she snuck out of San Francisco behind my back. By then she had remembered everything, of course, and she couldn't stand it.

"She was a proud creature. We must pay her that tribute at least. Give the devil her due. She told me once that if her illness got too bad, she would kill herself rather than just degenerate. I knew she meant it. I expected it, sooner or later.

"And yes, she did some speed. Not a lot. She went off it when it made her hallucinate again. I helped her.

"In fact, I helped her to survive longer than she might have done otherwise. And I wonder, my self-righteous old Ontario friend, just what *you* did for her?"

I'm hysterical, Ron thought, at last connecting with some more objective part of his consciousness. It was not euphoria that he had been experiencing all day, he realized, but some strange and hysterical delayed reaction to every-thing that had happened. I'm not in a rational condition to deal with this, or with anything, he thought. Yet here they were still climbing the dark stairs. Thank God he was not alone in this. There was Lester. He remembered now with trepidation that Lester was a stranger, a glad-handing American about whom he knew almost nothing. Upon whom he had projected his need for help. But Lester, thank God, had agreed to help. To guide him in this darkness. . . .

The plan was that together they would persuade Carl to talk to his father. Then they would get Carl and Ron on a flight to Canada. Ron knew that the hardest part would be whatever happened afterward, but he could not think about that now. It was one thing at a time.

I couldn't help Lisan. I may even have killed her. If I can't help him, what good am I?

The dark hallway once again. The green door with its patched and peeling paint.

Lester got to the door first. He knocked. He did not seem apprehensive. It was as if he helped to reclaim junkies every day.

There was no answer. Lester tried the door. It was not locked.

The dark apartment hallway inside. Then the room with the north light, the curved alcove window, the view of the bay and of Alcatraz. Again they were moving to the center of the maze. . . .

"Carl. Where are you, man?" calls out Lester cheer-fully.

The pink building still floats on the azure sky. A small crowd of people has gathered on the steep street below. Jackson Street. A police van is parked in front of the white front door. The people are waiting to see what, or who, will be carried out this time.

Above the street the police are going about their business.

"Okay. That'll do for now. Don't go anywhere."

Ron would be happy never in his life again to have to talk with a policeman. He is finished talking now.

While Lester is questioned in his turn Ron goes to the window and looks out to the bay. The water is a sparkling, innocent blue. The prison a dark shape. He remembers the frisking black seals in the blue ocean. What he feels is vertigo.

With another part of his mind he hears everything that Lester tells. It is almost all true. Like Ron, Lester says he has no idea just who might have been the "dealer" who made possible the "overdose".

After what seems to be a not very long interrogation Lester joins him at the window. The two policemen have resumed their close examination of the premises.

Lester says: "We couldn't have done nothing, man. Carl, he was wasted."

TEN

◆

Ron,
You will wonder why I did what I'm about to do. Thus this
letter. By the time you read this I will be gone. I owe you
this. This time around.

The waters are calling me.

I began to hallucinate when I was twelve. I don't believe
I ever did as a child. Unless I've blotted it out.

I had an imaginary lover. He was blond and small but
compact and muscular. We didn't make love but we'd be
naked and hug a lot. I think he was about eighteen. His
body was almost entirely hairless. I would spend whole
afternoons in my head with him. We would go to the spot
in the woods behind the beach, you know the one. I
stopped seeing my real friends. I stopped eating for a while
too. Till the doctor said they should send me away to
school. He said I had a morbid imagination and needed
discipline, order.

I called him Sandy. He had curly reddish blond hair on
his head and cute freckles. Odd — later on Carl looked a
bit like him, though I never thought of that till afterwards.

At school I kept seeing him. On the grounds. In the gym working out on the parallel bars. He was a superb gymnast who for some reason had to practice in secret at a Catholic girls' school. It was absurd. At night he would come to my bed and my roommate wouldn't wake up.

I learned to pretend to be alert even when I was seeing him. After my experience with the doctor I decided never to tell anyone again.

But then I began to see other people as well. Threatening strangers. A dark boy (I now think maybe he was you). A hostile old woman. A black man with a baseball bat. A crazy nun who carried a butcher knife in her robe. In fact, some of the nuns *were* rather weird; they had strange superstitions, especially about sex. I thought then it must be the school itself. I phoned Angelo at his apartment and asked him to help me get away from there. He wouldn't then. But he felt guilty. He got a psychiatrist to come and see me.

The hallucinations were especially bad during my period. But I was afraid to stay in bed, afraid to be left alone with my visions.

I didn't think then that I was "sick". I thought I had been "hexed" by an enchanter. Or punished for being "unclean" — as the nuns had promised us we would be. Please don't laugh at this. I mean it.

I have to tell you about Angelo or you'll never understand. All this about the visions is an evasive action. It's the truth but it's an evasion. A symptom. The psychiatrist told me that but he never got anywhere with me.

Angelo wanted to test the limits of things. He thought I should explore my madness as he was exploring his power over other people. At the same time he felt guilty about drawing me into his world at all. But he also wanted to hurt our parents, through me, if necessary. It was complicated.

Did you know our father made his money in chemicals? The war made him rich. I suppose he was a profiteer. They called him a patriot.

Father always blamed Angelo for not being quick. He abused him for not doing well in school. Basically he disliked his powerful but slow Italian brute of a son and drove him away. Mother didn't like him either. She had married to escape all things Italian and he was a constant reminder. She had wanted a girl. I think she made Angelo feel he was defective. So he rebelled. He came to hate them both. But he loved me. In his way. Insofar as he was capable of love. And I loved him to distraction. He was the dark enchanter of my young life.

When I was twelve and had begun to menstruate he took me to that Canadian beach one day and then back in among the trees. There he raped me.

I say "rape" but I didn't resist. I didn't want it but I didn't resist. I had no thought of sex but I loved him. I was always hugging him, so maybe I invited it in a way. He wanted to know what it would be like to do it with his twelve-year-old sister, I think. Just once. He was like that. I could never have refused him anything then. Later I got angry even though I was still financially dependent on him.

He liked to kill. He developed a taste for it. He liked to dominate other men. He despised and hated and — of course — *feared* women. Except perhaps for me. I found out all this when I left school a few years later. He set me up in an apartment and paid the rent. My parents were upset and angry. The hallucinations had stopped by then. Though they came back later in California.

He deflowered me in a more or less ritual way. He said it was his privilege because he was my older brother. He said that was what they did in Sicily. The father or the older brother. He kept talking all the time he was doing it until he began to shudder and collapse all over me. It was painful. There was a lot of blood.

After that the hallucinations started. And I couldn't eat. I wanted to blot out that powerful heavy body that had covered me and hurt me, the feel of all that hair on my skin. I wanted to cleanse myself.

Years later I learned to like sex. But I couldn't love. And it made me hate him.

Odd. I once thought that you were like me. But this summer it's different.

Your mother is right. To achieve freedom there must be a death. Angelo's death freed me for a time.

In California the hallucinations came back. I was popping quite a lot of amphetamines then. And I began to see Angelo on the street outside my apartment. When I was high I thought maybe he had come back to get me.

I also saw Larry. I mean I really saw him, he was there. But I don't want to talk about that.

I thought that maybe by coming back here I could get calm again. I thought maybe you would help. And I am calm now, in a way. But I'm no good for you, and you can't help me any more. Even if you weren't going to leave me, it would work out badly. Even though I had thought you were like me in some way.

I think the only time I haven't been seeing things is when I'm in bed with you.

The waters are so powerful and wise. All summer I've been looking at them. In California I kept seeing them. I guess that's really why I came back.

I thought for a while this summer I was pregnant. But I wasn't. Maybe I can't be. I had a crude abortion in Frisco. If I was pregnant it might make a difference.

I belong with Angelo. I think we were both born broken.

She put the letter in an envelope, sealed it, and wrote his name on it.

She wondered now if all of the story she had told was true. She wasn't sure she knew any more. She had lived with it, in it, so long. . . .

The waters are calling me.

She put the envelope under a large stone on the counter of the information booth. She was alone, the other girls were at lunch. He would be coming by at four. End of shift.

She walked down the little hill toward Table Rock House. It was one of those days when the fine mist was lifted high on the wind and made rainbows. Everything wavered a little in the heat. It was all beautiful and all quite unreal. Day's furnace. . . .

It will be cool, she thought. Cool and cruel. Cruel only to be kind. *Hamlet*. And the nuns. Ophelia. Ophelia, Sister Mary said, had gone mad because of impure thoughts. Her flowers. "There's rue. There's rosemary for remembrance." Floating violently. Down. She felt a little giddy.

She had to wait before she could cross the road to Table Rock House. There was a press of traffic and of people. She saw several nuns. Black-habited. Black ugly birds.

All ghosts, she thought.

She is wearing her tourist information uniform. I can see her always, quite distinctly. A white blouse and a dark-blue skirt. White for purity, white for water. White for life and for death. An absolute.

I want to be broken and made whole again.

She walked around Table Rock House and across the

other lane of the road. There were numbers of people, as usual, by the railing beyond which the wide white and green and blue water reached and stretched itself like some luxuriant multicolored snake over the edge. And down. A lover with flowing golden skin. She closed her eyes for a moment, listened, felt the spray on her cheek.

Then she walked along by the railing till she had reached a place a little way up from the brink where she could be alone.

An August day. The voices of the marrying rock and water made her feel calm, invulnerable. Free. Freedom is found close to the edge of things. She took off her high-heeled shoes.

Felicia, said the waters. Delicious, Felicia.

Lisan, she said aloud. My name is Lisan. *Listen.*

She climbed the railing. Nobody saw her at first.

She stepped into the cool green stream. Was wrenched off her feet. Instantly.

Pain. And glory. Ophelia, she thought, her mind close to the speed of light, her back broken by rocks. Until, in a kind of eternal slow motion, she fell and fell. . . .

Villanelle for Lisan

If you are fire and I am always rain
we cannot have identical desire;
we know a different quality of pain.

And now the brief, fierce summer burns again,
the white and wavering focus we require —
if you are fire and I am always rain —

it blurs our limbs and burns away their stain
in searing waves; that instant we aspire
we know a different quality of pain.

The crushed and crumpled grass where we have
    lain
fuses together all we should admire
if you are fire and I am always rain,

but green is choked with fall. And we remain
still full of our distinctness in the fire;
we know a different quality of pain.

So I must drown my fever to be sane,
defend us in the splendor of desire.
O you are fire and I am always rain.
We know a different quality of pain.

ELEVEN

◆

(The set is rather garish, with loud colors, bright-blue rugs and flamboyant orange curtains, and antique chairs that look as if you could not sit on them without destroying them. As the lights come up, Larry is discovered standing with his right arm stretched languorously along the mantel over an attractive but apparently unusable brick fireplace. He is wearing white trousers, a bright–blue sleeveless shirt, and a red scarf around his neck. The scarf conceals an outsize Adam's apple. He also has a trim beard that gives him a slightly nautical appearance. He wears light make-up to lessen the impact of a prominent scar.)

LARRY:

I suppose *Vertigo* is the best film ever shot in San Francisco. Some even think it the best Hitchcock, though it was not awfully well received at the time. As I recall. But so it goes. I saw it first in Sacramento. Loved it.

Twice James Stewart follows Kim Novak up the winding stair of a Spanish bell-tower—though heights make him dizzy, give him vertigo. It didn't occur to me at the time, but I wonder now if Hitchcock was remembering how Joseph Cotten followed Marilyn Monroe up the stairs of that other bell-tower back in my long-lost Canadian hometown. There he strangled her. (Pause) Only on screen, to be sure.

But *Vertigo* is, of course, a vastly superior film. And Kim Novak, not otherwise remembered as an actress of much merit, is surprisingly good in what amounts to two separate parts. When asked about her abilities, Hitchcock is reported to have said, "She didn't spoil the picture." Really. I ask you. Her mysterious, almost zombie-like beauty and, later, her tough vulgarity contributed greatly to it, I'd venture. In my humble opinion. But then Hitchcock is also supposed to have pronounced: "Actors are cattle."

Actors have to do what their directors tell them. And the characters they play are puppets of their scheming, dreaming authors.

It is in that spirit that my remarks must be understood, I'm afraid. Though perhaps I can attempt to sneak by the puppet-master from time to time some few observations of my very own. When, like Homer, he is nodding.

You probably think I'm fairly despicable. I suppose I can't blame you. But you haven't had to live my life.

I don't want to be maudlin about it. I passed through that phase some time ago. I don't want to indulge myself so far, though I still have my lapses, I fear.

It's a truism by now, isn't it, that everything important begins in childhood?

Well.

I had parents and a brother. They were all quite ordinary. But my father was killed in the war. I don't remember him very well.

We were not well off. We lived in a fairly cramped

apartment — one floor of a cheap wooden house on Centre Street — and I wore patched-up hand-me-down
clothes for as far back as I can remember. How I hated
them — especially the corduroy breeches of that dreadful
postwar period. Ugh. I have no doubt I wore hand-me-
down diapers in my playpen. My brother was just a year
older than I was.

I slept with my brother for years. He was always bigger
than I was. He protected me from bullies at school. When
he was around. (Pause) When he wasn't beating up on me
himself. He was a jock from birth. I was not. I was passive,
dreamy. Not good at games. Not good at anything, really,
till the kindly Grade Three teacher, Miss Byers — she had
the most enormous knockers, or should I say udders, that I
have ever seen — well, anyhow, Miss Byers told me one
day how well I sang. She *was* nice, she was the one non-
crabby teacher in the school. I was genuinely surprised
when she said it, singing was just something I liked to do.
It came naturally.

My mother liked me to sing. I could sing any song by,
say, the Andrews Sisters, word-perfect and note-perfect,
once I'd heard it a couple of times on the radio. Now the
Andrews Sisters sang some pretty silly songs — full of
baby-talk. At school they gave us old songs like "The
Swazi Warrior", "Danny Boy", and "Santa Lucia" (a
Caribbean island I have since visited, but it was then just an
exotic, mispronounced name to us).

My mother and I would sing together while she
washed the dishes and I dried them. She liked old Irish
songs, the sadder the better. She was a sentimental slob.

I suppose she might have married again except for us.
Me. I was very demanding, I'm sure. I demanded all of her
attention. My brother — Albert — was more independent.

He was always off playing some sport or other after
school. But I always came straight home. I didn't really
have friends.

I remember Ronnie Benson came over one day to trade
comics. We read some together and started giggling and
laughing together on the back steps. For some reason
(because I felt like it just then, I guess, and even though I
almost never saw him out of school) I said, "You know, I
think you're my best friend."

He stopped laughing. He fixed me with that oh-so-
serious, earnest, and baleful look he often had. *Has.*
"You're not *my* best friend," he announced. "Carl Palmer
is *my* best friend."

I didn't even *like* him that much, anyway.

It was later that I fell in love. It was near the end of what
we called public school.

I fell in love with Steve Hendricks.

This took some getting used to. I was twelve or so, I
guess. I had always assumed, like every boy, that I would
fall in love with a girl. That's what you did. A girl much
like my mother. I'd marry her some day. I even thought, in
Grade Three or maybe Four, that I *was* in love with Ann
Bolt. She was, of course, like all the girls, in love with Steve.
Or shall I say, as we did then, she "liked" him. I knew she
could never take me seriously. But I thought she was the
prettiest and smartest girl in our class. The girls all tried to
get good marks; the boys pretended they didn't care.

Because I invited Ann to a birthday party once, she had
to invite me to one of hers. When we played spin-the-
bottle she got to kiss Steve. As it happened. Everybody
knew she liked him. They seemed made for each other.

Boys and girls could only come together at parties or
other social rituals of an established kind. School dances,
say. Mostly the guys moved in a pack. Everyone looked to

Steve the athlete as the natural leader. At school I hung around him as much as I could. From Grade One on. I was never one of the popular kids, but he suffered me.

Maybe I was always in love with him.

He was basically kind. He was my brother all over again. Only nicer.

This is boring. It's boring even me. I'll skip ahead. You don't want to see me cry.

The point is, I suffered for several years the pangs of a love that, as they say, could never speak its name (Steve being straight to the point of paralysis), let alone be requited.

It made me very unhappy.

And the others gave me a hard time. Particularly Carl. He could always get Steve to laugh at some mean joke at my expense. I pretended to be a good sport sometimes. Sometimes I slunk away.

Carl was the joker in the pack. Carl, a bit later on, took to calling Rock Hudson and Doris Day "the fag and the blob". For we all knew, even in the fifties, that old Rock was gay. As for Doris, she was "the blob" because they photographed her in very soft, buttery-blonde focus. Those were the days. My rotten salad days.

I got into a phase where I was sexually attracted to half of the guys around. Even including Carl, who was increasingly good-looking, and whom I sometimes hated.

Then, finally, I found a friend. Imagine. In that dreary town. It was a kind of miracle.

I had heard, of course, about "Old Queen Harold". They said he hung around the YMCA dances on Saturday nights and offered guys rides home afterwards. He organized the dances.

Normally I never went to these. Girls weren't attracted to me. They would dance with me only with obvious reluctance. But one Saturday night I was so bored, so restless, that I went out for a walk. I found myself headed in the direction of the Y.

It was late. When I looked in the ballroom door the central revolving, kaleidoscopic colored lights were moving over the dim faces and bodies of the huddled slow-dancers, and they were playing Glenn Miller's "Moonlight Serenade" — always the last record, the last dance, here. I was alone in the doorway. Many kids would already have gone home; it was the couples, confirmed or maybe just getting together, who were left.

Someone came up behind me in the doorway. I did not turn to see who it was. I was, perversely, masochistically even, watching the anonymous, presumably happy couples pressed up together.

A hand brushed against my rear. As if by accident. (I was slim in those days but with a quite nicely packed, rounded bum.) My heart jumped but I did not look. The hand returned. Casually at first. I allowed it. He was stroking me, feeling me. A few feet from the oblivious couples lost in flesh and moonlight. I let him. Then he said, softly, almost growling, "Come on. We'll go someplace more private. Connie will close up for me if I ask her."

He took me to the cemetery.

After that my life changed.

We went to Buffalo most Friday nights. (This is a tale of three cities.) I had to lie to my mother and my brother about where I was going. And with whom. I had been such a stay-at-home. But my brother was always out himself. My mother thought I had a girlfriend; she said I should bring her home.

We went to bars in Buffalo. I met lots of people there.

There was a whole way of life, I could see. I visited it repeatedly. I wanted it.

Till I went and didn't come back.

How that happened is a painful story, I don't want to tell it. Except to say my brother caught on to me (I guess that was inevitable), and he exploded. He thought that *his* "honor" was at stake. The asshole.

I knew people who would put me up in Buffalo. Temporarily. While I looked for a job. When my bruises and black eye had healed enough that somebody might hire me, that is.

Harold later went to Toronto, I think. His cover was blown. I never saw him again. I had never loved him, I can hardly remember him. There was a hushed-up scandal, thanks to my not-too-bright brother's blabbing, a lot of talk about the kind of people who worked at the Y, but nothing in the local family newspaper, of course. (This was decades before they started publishing the names of men entrapped in shopping-mall washrooms by over-zealous police.) My mouthy brother told everyone he saw it was "good riddance to bad rubbish" if I was gone.

My mother had some kind of breakdown. She had always been nervous. They had to put her in a nursing home while she was still fairly young. Then they took her to the hospital and gave her shock treatments to shock her out of her depression. But later on she was hysterical and violent. They gave her a lobotomy for that. That was in the progressive 1950s, in London, Ontario. I discovered the gory details when, eventually, I tried to reach her. My brother said it was all my fault for being such a degenerate.

Not pretty.

I had been all she really cared about, I think. I think

maybe my brother was jealous, almost all his life, and now was having his revenge on her too.

I was under-age but the police never came after me. My mother was in no shape to insist on it. Everyone else was glad to be rid of me.

I worked first at menial jobs, mostly waiting on tables, then as a singer in bars. I was into jazz singing and ballads by then. I tried to sound like Johnny Mathis. I sang in the after-hours room of The Wild Side. That's where Angelo first saw me.

At first I liked his attentions. He spent money on me, bought me things. He leaned on the management, who were always incredibly deferential to him, to raise my salary. As a singer I was enjoying my first experience of being thought especially desirable: the ugly duckling transformed. I didn't appreciate for quite a while that Angelo would want to end my career, take my life over completely, and deny me any other lovers. He was serious, he wanted a little wifey. I was fairly promiscuous then — also something of a drunk and at least an apprentice junkie. It all went with the territory. The underground of the American dream. Where musicians and blacks and gangsters and queers and addicts and other outlaws often overlapped and congregated. This was the dark side of the moon, the side *Guys and Dolls* didn't sing about.

I had hoped I might make it to Vegas. Or Hollywood. Or New York. With Angelo's help, his muscle and his money. But that wasn't what he had in mind.

Angelo was not your garden-variety hood, mind you. He had taste and some degree of intelligence. He came from a good family. I am perversely proud of that still.

He perfected my taste for being fucked in the ass. You laugh. (Pause) Don't knock it.

Where was I?

Angelo. Well. What is there to be said? He was a second-generation entrepreneur. His father had made *his* money in chemicals. So did Angelo, partly. Only different chemicals. It was perhaps just a logical development. The American dream all over again.

And Lisan. She was Felicia then. She was a knock-out. I've heard it said that homosexuals appreciate female beauty more perfectly than any "normal" male can do. She was an objet d'art. She could not have lived to be old.

She was my relief from Angelo. When he got too heavy. Those times when I wanted to escape from him. We plotted ways that I might run away. And how, with his connections and resources, he might find me. How he would certainly kill me in some slow, sadistic way when he did.

It was a sick game. Felicia was a rather sick girl. We'd smoke dope together. Sometimes take stronger things. Uppers. She'd tell me about her hallucinations. Her bouts of madness, as they say. I told her all about my home-town and my childhood. She said it sounded like a fantasy. She said it sounded quaint, sweet, safe. Like an old farming community in Iowa. She said she could almost smell the corn. Or was it the shredded wheat growing in the fields? And we'd both laugh our heads off at that one.

The night Angelo died was just the latest of many such nights, over those two or three years. Or however long it was. It seemed an eternity at the time. An eternity of bondage. Of what I loved and what I hated.

I was a sick boy.

I was gone, I was crying. Ron Benson came in like a hallucination from the distant past. The night before, when I saw *all* of them, including Steve (how that tore my heart), seemed already a million years ago. I had made sure of that — with booze, dope, sex with different guys.

All that was on my mind now was Angelo. Whom I

loved and I hated. When he phoned I went home.

What happened then? I just bet you think you know. But why does it have to be me who did it? *Everybody* hated him. I mean *everybody.*

Maybe I wish I had, though.

Maybe the Canadian worm turned. Is that surprising?

Maybe it was an accident. A "play" that got out of hand.

Maybe it was somebody else. Like Lisan's "contract" of the previous year.

I really don't remember any more. Believe me.

As for me, suh, *ah* lit out for the territory. So to speak. Went west, as a young man must. Eventually I fetched up here. A tale of three cities.

How I live here it would be, uh, indiscreet to divulge. I have had, let us say, many instructive adventures. Maturing experiences. I have prospered. But my sins are many. (Did you know I once taught Sunday school? When I was fifteen?)

And of course my past came back. To haunt me. In the shape of luscious Lisan. Of Carl the golden boy. My childhood tormenter. He was here for years before I ran into him. He was such a knock-out now I didn't even recognize him. I was rather stoned at the time.

He told me Lisan was here. I found her. Before she might find me. She was rather the worse for wear by then. Poor thing. I kept a friendly eye on her. Till she slipped away.

As for Carl, I merely assisted at his self-punishment. Each of us is responsible for his own life. His own downfall. Oh. I'll admit this much. I was not averse to a little revenge. A worm will always turn when it gets the chance. Carl could serve my needs if he wanted my product. When he got too weak to do me properly, I did him a few times. I like to take the active role occasionally just to remind myself that I can. But eventually he wasn't so pretty any more. It was a shame.

He'd have overdone it sooner or later anyway. He's the addictive type. I gave him a large, free supply that time so he couldn't run out on me. He was usually too high to function. I wanted him here. I thought Ron might pop him into a hospital, and while he was there I would work on old Ron. Ply him with pills, freebies, and stories about Lisan. He was obsessed with her. Keep him here too, perhaps indefinitely. A little colony of expatriates. High all the time.

(Or is this all just a fantasy of the puppet-master? I suspect he'll never know.)

When I learned Carl was dead I went to L.A. and disappeared for a year. (I'm good at disappearing, I'm invisible in a crowd.) I shaved off my beard. Just to be on the safe side. Nothing happened. Ron must have kept his mouth shut about me.

Eventually I came back. I like it better here. L.A. is too . . . too modern for me, I guess. I'm Canadian.

Sometimes I think it's all been a dream. It began in the field of long grass where I watched Steve and Carl jerking off at recess. Urging each other on. My own organ stiffening in sympathy. They talked about tits and ass, while I thought about the two of them. I thought of them in bed together.

Sometimes I think I've been floating in a night world all my life. It's not the real world, it's a fantasy. I'm somebody's hallucination.

I can't remember when I last left this room. I'm not sure there even *is* a door. The fireplace doesn't work, it's bricked-up somewhere. I've been snorting up. A while ago. So my mind wanders a little. There's someone in the bedroom. Watching television. But I can't remember his name just now.

It all began in the field of long grass. A few minutes ago. I don't know how it ends. The earthquake or the bomb, I guess.

All that water falling off a cliff. As Oscar Wilde is supposed to have said, it would be truly marvelous if it went the other way. *That* would give one a touch of the vertigo.

Sometimes, now, I think Lisan had the right idea. And Marilyn too.

Anyway, the cliff is unavoidable. The fall. Endless. As if there were no bottom to reach. As if the world is, finally, one bottomless, limitless dark. A hell of the imagination. The hell of the puppet-master.

Anyhow. Everything falls away. Every last thing. . . .

I'm fading now.

(Indeed the lights have been dimming for several minutes. This creates a murky, underwater effect.)

Everything falls away. So fast. In the twinkling of an eye. In the fall of the sparrow, the turn of the dragonfly's wing. Many of us are damaged on the way, some destroyed. All eventually disappear. . . .

Hell is everywhere. . . .

No reversal, no turning back.

Just this.

This falling and falling away. . . .

(Silence. Blackout.)

TWELVE

◆

"He was not . . ." — here he paused momentarily — "quite what I expected."

"How was he?" asked Harriet. What else could she say?

"Just a very calm, very quiet old man. Not senile. Just slow and calm. Not at all the terror I expected."

"How sad," she said. "I don't think I want to see him defeated."

"I'm not sure that he is," said Ron. "He's simply grown very calm. As if he had known it all. All passion spent."

"That's Milton?" she queried.

"Yes."

"I was once quite well read in the classics," said Harriet. "He saw to that."

She was affected, he could see, by news of her father. But she did not know how to respond. She had rejected a man who seemed no longer to exist. She should perhaps have known, have expected this.

Ron had gotten in touch with his grandfather through his godmother Alice, his mother's cousin. Alice told him she had always thought, especially as the years passed, that

Harriet was rather "hard" about her father. When Ron had arranged a meeting by phone one day he told his mother. She could not object. He said that he wanted to know as much as he could about where he came from. It was all he had to hold on to now.

"People are so rootless now, so lost, caught up in the industrial process. Or else aimless wanderers. Like . . ." And he paused.

"He was rooted all right," said Harriet. "He's probably still quite capable of telling you about the family farm — ad nauseam."

But Harriet could not object to her son's finally seeking out his grandfather. For one thing, it gave him a purpose. After the deaths of Lisan and then Carl, he had seemed incapable of concentrating on anything. He didn't work, he didn't do anything that she could see. Brooding on family history would at least divert him from his recent disasters. It would also get him away from the house and force him to deal with the external world again. She did not want him on her hands forever.

She had indulged his depression and bad nerves for two months since his return from California. He had rarely left the house in that time. It was time for him to *do* something. At least he still wrote letters to a girl from Toronto who was now in England. She was not a disturbed American. Sooner or later, surely, he would go there. And Harriet could get on with her own renewed life.

"He said he knew that he had been too hard on you. But he couldn't at first forgive you for eloping. Later he didn't know how he could make things right again. He thought that by then you wouldn't want him in your life."

"I didn't," said Harriet.

His grandfather Listowel was in a wheelchair. They sat in a small "crafts" room by themselves near a large window that looked out on a garden made bright by late-fall sunshine.

"I look out this window a lot," the old man said. "The others don't come here very much, so I often have the place to myself. I don't really care for the television going or the crowds in the big room."

The "others" mostly lounged or chattered or dozed in a large reception room with a television set which was always on but which scarcely anyone really watched. Some of them made loud, senile noises. Animal cries of distress, Ron thought. He found the room depressing even to walk through. There was also a woman passing through, an old woman obviously demented but with a face that must once have been lovely, who did nothing — he was later told — but walk, very jerkily, with one shoulder hitched up above the other, along the corridors all day. Jerking round and round the building. Every day: the futile, unvaried round. Sometimes, though, she would stop to ask someone where her husband was. He had recently died on the "outside". For some reason the old woman stayed in Ron's mind.

Reverend Listowel was now a thin, rather short man without much hair left on the top of his head. His face was pink and wrinkled — really quite benign-looking. He was neatly dressed in a suit; he would obviously disdain to live out his last days in pyjamas or a dressing-gown like some of the "others". Or perhaps the suit was only because of the visit? He did not wear a tie. Arthritis had crippled the old man some ten years before. It must be difficult to get him dressed. But he seemed to bear his tribulations with patience.

"I'm still able to read a good part of the day," he told his grandson. "That takes me out of myself. And I listen to a transistor radio that Alice gave me. I can do that without disturbing anyone else."

When Ron had first entered his room the old man had said, "Are you my grandson then?"

"Yes. The younger one."

"Sit down. No. We'll go into the sitting–room. What I call my sitting–room. Then we can look at the garden."

There was another old man dozing in his bed at the farther end of the small room. The room was adequate, Ron decided, quite institutional, smelling as it did of disinfectant; it was functional, with its two beds, its closets, small bureaus, and adjoining bathroom. It was not, he thought, immediately depressing, but it was not exactly cheerful either. Someone had brought the other man some flowers.

The old man wheeled himself quite efficiently down the hall to the door of the "sitting–room". Ron followed. By the bright window he sat down in a chair facing his grandfather.

"Yes," said the latter. "You do have some of the Listowel look about you. The dark Celtic. I saw it as soon as you came into my room. But the light is better in here."

"I think I'm more like my mother than I am like my father."

"And how is your mother?" Reverend Listowel's tone seemed quite neutral.

Ron hesitated slightly. "She's well, I think. She's had to adjust and reorganize herself. My father died."

"I am sorry," said his grandfather. "Though I did not know him. But I'm afraid I probably misjudged him. I was certain at the time that such an impulsive match must work out badly." He sighed. And Ron felt an immediate relief that this subject had been admitted.

"He was, in fact, a very responsible and conscientious man," he said. "But I know the story of my parents' elopement, and its aftermath."

"Yes. It must seem very remote to you. It now seems very remote to me. I think I remember your mother better as a girl than as a young woman. No doubt I was to blame in wanting her to remain a girl. But she should have been more patient. Less headstrong. We are both stubborn, I'm afraid, it's in the Listowel blood. It made us good farmers in our time."

He seemed to be saying: it was all so long ago. His manner was so mild that Ron wondered if he could ever have been so stern as Harriet had said he was.

The old man sighed once again before he spoke.

"It's not for us to believe that we can finally direct events. That is the conclusion I have reached. Do you know that it has taken me most of my life to realize that? I mean, really to know it. It had always, of course, been what I taught my 'flock' — if that's the word for them. Who then, of course, asked *me* — not God — for direction. This is ironic."

"Perhaps you should write to my mother — to say some of these things."

The old man shrugged.

"Would she believe me? Would she want to hear them now? I've felt it was best to leave her alone, that that was what she wanted. Of course, now that she's a widow, she may feel differently. I don't know. But my hands don't work so well any more, you see. Oh no. I never write letters now. . . ."

His voice trailed off. For the first time Ron thought that his grandfather seemed a little vague. Or was he simply disinclined to change his situation in any way that might revive old emotions? Perhaps he simply tired easily. He was old.

"My greatest pleasure," Reverend Listowel suddenly announced, "is in the novels of Jane Austen. I never tire of rereading her. Do you know them?"

He had caught Ron off-guard. Was it just to change the subject?

"My niece Alice tells me that you are a student of literature," he continued.

"Yes. I've graduated."

"And what will you do now?" The voice was detached, smooth, bland, it was the voice of the minister taking an intelligent interest in the plans of the young.

"I don't know. Soon I'll need to get a job, for a while, anyhow. I'll work on the bridge again in the summer. And in the fall I'll travel in Europe, I think. After that, maybe graduate work."

"You are in no hurry, I see," said the old man slightly ironically. So that Ron felt just a hint of the minister's former authority. A hint of steel.

Somehow this gave him new strength.

He was unwilling to let the subject of his mother lapse. He wanted more from them. He wanted to bind up the broken links of the family chain: it was all he had now. The broken family. He wanted to revive it. Even revive old chains of bondage, since these could not simply be wished out of existence, they had to be acknowledged. Then there might be freedom. He felt he must persist. Even if he had to force this strangely calm old man to relive a deep pain. Even if he had to force his own mother to give up some of her new autonomy.

The words were simple. But they took all the energy he had. He would not speak them twice.

"Shall I ask my mother to come and see you?"

His grandfather looked away to the garden. The sunlit garden.

"You know," he said quietly, "that space out there reminds me of the back garden in the first house I ever owned. Harriet used to play in it when she was very small."

He sighed yet again. Ron saw that he was often sad. But calm.

Then he continued more slowly and deliberately.

"Everything passes and changes. Let me say the obvious. My daughter went away — all children do, one way or another. She had, and has, her own life. I can't, and don't wish to, disturb it. This is as it should be, and will be. But if she should wish to come, consent to come, I shall be happy to see her."

"I want," said Ron then, "to know more about the family. About old Ontario. Before it got so Americanized."

Ron told Harriet about all of this, gradually, in no special order.

Harriet went away to weep by herself. Then she returned.

"I knew, I think, that this would happen some day," she said. "That I would have to 'play the reconciliation scene'. I've resisted it for years, but I knew it."

"You'll feel better when you see him," said Ron.

"Perhaps. I think the worst thing will be admitting that about some things he was quite right. You know, I think, as your brother Michael probably never will, and perhaps never should, that I was wrong to marry your father."

"Yes. I know."

"Not that he wasn't a good man."

"Yes. He was."

"But it should have been different — at the time I was intoxicated with my own daring. It was a negative act."

A silence. What happened, happened, thought Ron. *I* happened.

"I guess this is the time to tell you, then," said Harriet.

"Tell me?"

"I'm going to marry Steven Hendricks. In the spring. He's asked and I've accepted him."

The widow and the widower. Studying their "great books" together each Tuesday. Coming close together over coffee afterwards. He could see it. Steve's father. And his mother. It was logical, a logical development. What happens, happens. But he was totally unprepared.

"I'll take him with me," said Harriet. "I'll take my new fiancé with me when I go to see my father."

Then they would have come full circle.

THIRTEEN

◆

(Steve is seated in his basement workroom. He is surrounded by power tools. He is about forty now. He is relaxing, smoking a cigarette. He wears a plaid workshirt and jeans. He is a little gray at the temples.)

STEVE:

Hi. I'm the square one. Steve.

For a start I want to say this. This is a *good* town. *I* like it here. I've never understood their restlessness. I have been happy enough here, all these years, with my wife and kids. *Happy.*

The job's okay too, I guess. Not exciting. But then whose is? It pays the bills. I never wanted to travel anywhere. Even Florida.

I'm the one who stayed home. When the rest of them took off. "That old gang of mine."

I'm a family man. My father even came to live with us for a while after my mother died. Till he remarried.

I mean, what's wrong with the place you grew up in, happily?

Those guys didn't know when they were well off.

My own story is simple, I guess.

My mom and dad were good folks. He owned a men's clothing store. You know, the solid-value old-fashioned kind, not the sort of flashy thing that came in by the late sixties. A good-value store. I guess they're all gone now.

My mother had a weak heart. Or she'd be alive today. We — my little sister and I — didn't know that when we were growing up. We took her for granted, as kids do.

My sister lives in Baltimore now with her husband and three kids. Every couple of years they come to visit. We've always gotten along fine. Our kids do too. I have a boy and a girl. My wife's name is Annie.

From school I remember, mainly, that I played baseball. In fact, I still play baseball. I never stopped. The company sponsors our team. The River Rats. We play mostly over the river, since it's technically an American team. But sometimes we play on this side and I get to play against guys I went to high school with. It keeps me in some kind of shape. Even if we put away a few beers afterwards. As we usually do.

These are my friends now. The guys I play with. And Mike at work. Otherwise my family takes up all my free time.

Oh, I see Ronnie when he visits with his mother. We have a barbecue or something. But he's a bit of a stranger now, though friendly enough. I know Mike much better. Ron lives in Toronto. He's been a teacher. He's also written books I've never tried to read. But I've never been much of a reader. Though I do like to read Louis L'Amour westerns when I'm on holiday. I find those books really absorbing

— it's another world. The only escape I ever need — to the old frontier. "Go west, young man."

My other early friends are, of course, long gone.

I guess they were a slightly strange bunch. I guess I can say that now.

Especially Larry. He was the first to leave. It shocked everybody. He ran away from home, and his mother had a nervous breakdown. She never got well again. They said he sang jazz in queer bars. They said he was the boyfriend of a queer hood in the Mafia. It all sounded fantastic to this town.

When we saw him in Buffalo that time, though, he was just pathetic. Really pathetic. No wonder — he was always so weedy, and everybody picked on him. Mostly in fun. But kids are cruel without realizing. I had to crack down on my own kids when they were young.

He had no father and he grew up queer. Sad. *And* he had a crush on me. I still find that embarrassing. Why?

Partly I suppose because I wonder if I couldn't have been a bit nicer to him. Though what difference would it have made? He was what he was. He'd have done it anyway.

All the time he was hanging around I'd rather not have been bothered with him. But he did hang around; so he was part of the gang, even if his main function was to be the butt of Carl's jokes.

Carl. He had a cruel streak. He was my best friend, though, certainly, for a while in our early teens.

What went wrong with *him*? It's rather hard to say. He had all the advantages. Everything going for him. His old man was a *doctor*, for Christ's sake. But he had a self-destructive streak, I guess. He needed to push everything to the limit. He was the kind of guy who can never be satisfied, who wants more and more excitement all the time.

My life has had lots of good times. Who needs that kind of excitement?

I don't know now what we thought we had in common — except at the time, mercifully fairly brief, when we were both desperate to get ourselves laid. That was our bond. That's when we were best friends and confided in one another. Later I was married young, while Carl ran around and around in circles just as fast as he could at home and in California.

(Pause)

He made off with Ronnie's girl. Who later jumped into the falls. I think old Ron was well out of that one. Just think if he'd married her. He was wildly in love with her, it seems. She was obviously even nuttier than Carl.

That time encouraged wildness. Somehow. Maybe it was left over from the war. It had to work itself out. That's why you got Elvis, Marilyn Monroe, Marlon Brando in his torn T-shirt or on a bike. The whole "beat" thing. James Dean.

Well, I don't want all that back. My kids can watch *Happy Days* all they like. "The Fonz" — that totally fake biker. I'll take right now.

Ron. He was always moody. They say he's been in hospital from time to time for depression or anxiety or something. He doesn't talk about it to me, though. He's always very even now, maybe too even to be true. Washed-out, in some way. He should play a sport, it'd do him no end of good.

But he's an intellectual, I guess. A deep thinker. His wife, whom I don't feel I really know, always looks a bit frazzled, worried. She chain-smokes even though *he* is dead against smoking. She's nice enough, but a little distant. She thinks we're boring, I guess.

I like to smoke at times myself, but in moderation. Just like I like to drink beer. It's relaxing.

I *am* boring, I know. So it goes. Even my dreams are boring. Except . . . once. . . . Yeah.

Once, a number of years ago, I dreamed that Carl was alive again. I don't know why, I didn't often think about him. (I think about the past more now, God knows why, I suppose I'm getting middle-aged.) Anyhow, in this particular dream he had come to see me. I was really surprised to see him there on the doorstep. Big as life, smiling crookedly. I thought you were dead, I said. No, no, he said. He was smiling broadly, crazily. He was always joking. Remember that time, he said. What time? You know, he said. He was . . . well, insinuating. Then I woke up.

The wife was away with the kids visiting her folks at their cottage for a week. And I was missing her sexually. Quite badly. I was alone in our bed that morning. In fact, I woke up with an erection. But no Annie beside me. Troubled — just a little. The dream bothered me. I'd have forgotten it right away, I think, if I hadn't been alone. But it nagged me through breakfast.

Remember that time . . . What time?

Then all at once, after breakfast, when I was glancing quickly at the headlines of the *Globe and Mail* before getting dressed for work, it came to me. I remembered something I had totally forgotten for years. It's just a little embarrassing to tell. Though natural — pretty normal for that age, I believe. Though if my son, now a bit older, has had a similar experience, I don't really want to know about it.

It was our horny period. We were thirteen, fourteen? We talked and talked endlessly about sex. We had never, either of us, been laid. We thought of nothing much else. (Except sports.) We looked for "dirty" books to read (without buying them) at the corner drugstore. One real jim-dandy, I recall, was called *He Learned About Women.* We got off on the stuff that happened in these books — usually one sexual encounter per chapter. It's a little embarrassing now because they were basically pretty silly. The authors were often enjoying themselves — as in the scene where the innocent young hero just happens to meet a bare-breasted woman in the woods and she squirts milk in his eye with her huge left tit.

Well . . . it's nothing, I suppose. But I'll tell it. To show I can laugh at myself. One night Carl slept over at my house while his parents were away on a brief vacation. We couldn't get to sleep because we were entertaining each other, as usual, with talk about tits and ass and in particular a well-endowed girl at school named Judy Barnes. I was thinking also about Marilyn Monroe. About seeing her in the flesh. Till I had a huge rod-on. I said, if you were a girl I'd rape you right here and now, and rolled over on top of him. (Needless to add, my parents were out somewhere till quite late that night.) He entered right into the spirit of this. We were wrestling, sort of. I was always the stronger. We were rubbing our bodies, our bare chests together. Until, in quite short order, we both came tumultuously in our pajama-bottoms. It was a bit of a sticky mess afterwards.

So there you are. My one queer experience in forty years. Come back to haunt me. And *I* took the initiative too. Goes to show you.

Afterwards we said nothing. We rolled apart. Came unstuck. We slept right away. It never happened again. We didn't talk about it in the morning, or any time. We went on as if nothing had happened. And in a way nothing had. The very next month I lost my virginity with a girl named

Myra Stone. She lived next door. Carl did it later, I think, with Jane Berners, who was kind of the town whore.

But he was the one who became the ladies' man. I had a steady girl after a couple of years and then got married young. Well, I got her pregnant. But we would have got married eventually anyway, I'm sure. I've never regretted it.

When I realized, that morning, what the dream-Carl wanted to remind me of, I started to laugh, I couldn't help it. Goddam horny teenagers, I thought. They'll fuck the dog if they're horny enough. And I laughed and laughed. The little tension that the dream had aroused was all gone.

I'm sorry, Carl, I said to his ghost, but it's funny. I can't help it, it's funny. I don't mean it's funny you're dead. I'm still sorry you're dead. Really I am.

But I couldn't stop laughing. Laughing and laughing my ass off.

FOURTEEN

◆

The stomach ache began one morning in late June. A pain in the left side of my stomach. I thought it would go away and so I went in to work on the bridge. I was living then in my mother and stepfather's new house in a subdivision on the escarpment several miles out of town. I was again a customs officer at the Canadian end of the Rainbow Bridge. The bridge that married two huge countries.

The pain grew worse all morning, so I decided to take the day off and go home. I had had a lift in with Mr. Hendricks but now had to take a bus home. I felt steadily worse.

I had always had a slightly nervous stomach. So my mother was not inclined to take this present malaise very seriously. She got me some Pepto-bismol, and I went to bed.

There I slept only fitfully. And dreamed dreams.

I am in Larry's apartment again. It is garish in decor, loud colors, bright–blue rugs, flamboyant curtains, and antique furniture.

Larry is seated by the attractive but unusable brick fireplace and is smiling at me in a subtly hostile manner.

He is saying: "You shouldn't have killed me, you know. It only makes me stronger. I'll get you for it, you know."

"Did I kill you?" I know that I am dreaming, but I am not sure what I have done, or in what world.

"You forced an overdose on me. Just what I did to Carl."

"No," I hear myself correcting him, "summary or frontier justice is an *American* bad habit. Canadians believe in due process of law."

I am standing, somewhere in time, by the edge of the falls. It is the American side. I notice now a bald middle-aged man standing beside me. He is wearing a gray business suit. He is emptying a vial of some strange yellowish liquid over the edge.

"I've come down from Buffalo," he confides. His manner might be called chummy. His face has a look of insane good cheer — like a Shriner, a little drunk, at a convention.

"I'm poisoning the waters," he says brightly.

"You're Lisan's father."

"I'm the king of the poisoned river. I'm poisoning the well."

I say: "The thunder-god will get you for this. Your children will be cursed and damned. The Neutrals will have their revenge."

He only smiles then. He says, quietly, "Vengeance is mine."

I am standing over Larry's body. His throat is cut. He is bleeding profusely, still alive though barely, making vivid red pools on the loud violet carpet.

I say, "This is what you did to Angelo."

In the forest it is very dark. You can hear the falls roaring softly in the background. You can see, gradually, some dark, semi-naked figures moving among the trees. Indians. Or else spirits of the wood. A tall man has emerged a little out of darkness and is beckoning. I go to him.

"Lester," I say.

"Follow me, man."

He leads me through the wood. There is a barely discernible path. Soon the trees and the undergrowth are denser, more difficult to negotiate. It is a labyrinth.

I am falling behind.

"Lester," I call out. But he is gone.

Around me in the forest I can hear the fighting now. Men are killing other men. There are cries and gunshots.

Then there is a sudden clearing. The center of the maze. It is lighter here. Faint dawnlight.

Angelo is tied to a tree. The Indians are disemboweling him with their small hatchets. His guts, his intestines and blood, are jerking out in lurid red ropes and coils that seem endless. Though his mouth is open he makes no sound. Perhaps they have cut out his tongue already.

"No," I say softly. I am sorry for the monster.

Somewhere I hear Lester singing. He has a deep baritone voice. Like Paul Robeson. He is singing "Old Man River".

In the clearing there is also a little hill. On it stands Lisan. She is quite naked. She is Queen of the Hill. Her body is painted in red and blue colors — like the colored lights on the falls. She is smiling now, triumphantly.

I woke up with a start. In pain. The pain was much worse. I've got to go to the hospital, I thought.

I found my mother reading in the living-room with its large picture-window. There was a view of the country-side below the hill and in the distance Lake Ontario. On a clear day you could see Toronto. Harriet's marriage, I thought witlessly, has broadened her social horizons.

"I think I'd better go to Emergency," I said. "This is getting worse."

"Are you sure?" said my mother. The Listowels had never held with making a fuss about minor illnesses like flu or the common cold.

I saw then as well how much my mother wanted to remain calm and collected. She wanted peace and quiet, not another crisis.

"Yes," I said. "The medicine hasn't helped. If anything, it's made it worse."

Soon Mr. Hendricks came home, only to have to leave again immediately to take me to the hospital. What a nuisance I am to them, I thought. They'll be glad when I'm gone.

In the car I found myself picturing the whirlpool. Everything, I thought, sooner or later approaches that bright beckoning vortex.

We sat waiting our turn in the crowded emergency room. The wait seemed endless. There were women with crying children, men with no obvious immediate complaint, one accident victim whose bloody head had gone through a windshield. She was soon taken away.

Eventually an intern came to look at me. He's just an apprentice doctor, I thought. In fact he was Billy Carpenter, who had been only three years ahead of me in high school.

Billy poked and prodded at my stomach.

"Does it hurt?"

"Yes. Constantly."

"You're not reacting much."

"It hurts."

I had always been taught not to complain, not to react too much to pain.

They took a blood sample just to decide whether anything was seriously wrong.

More waiting. Fifteen minutes, half an hour. The pain remained steady.

Billy returned.

"You're highly infected," he said. "It can only be appendicitis. So we're going to admit you."

"And operate?"

"Possibly."

I was admitted, I signed a paper permitting them to operate, I was put to bed. I was not allowed to eat.

The walls of the room were a yellowy cream color. There was a man in the other bed but he was asleep.

I thought for a moment of my grandfather's shared room in the nursing–home. My thoughts were wandering now. I was groggy from pain.

The walls of the room had an ambiguous yellow quality. A color that would change with the light. I had noticed this before when . . .

Yes. My father.

Maybe this is even the same room.

My father is standing at the foot of the bed. He is all dressed in white. Like Dr. Palmer, Carl's father. Perhaps they are the same.

We are walking on the grass near Table Rock House. My father the doctor and me. Across the road, the gleaming white falls. It is twilight.

"You'll have to come with me, I'm afraid," says my father in his tired voice of that last summer. "I'm sorry, but that's the way it is."

"But why?"

"You aren't meant to have any more time. You belong to a doomed generation. They're going to drop the bomb quite soon, you know."

I protest: "But the lost generation was in the 1920s. Your generation." It seems unfair.

"You'll like it here," says my father. "Things are clearer. Once you're here. It's only the passage that's difficult."

"I want to come, I think. Don't I?"

"Yes," says my father. "You want to come."

My father's face is all light, really quite beautiful. Strange, I think, he was never terribly handsome. But he looks like an older version of Carl now.

I woke up for a moment then. I located myself. Here in the hospital bed. But something was very strange now. I felt so peaceful. No pain. Yes. There was no pain any more.

It had gone, receded as I slept. I was immensely tired, I wanted to sleep and sleep. But what a relief it was to realize that the pain was gone. Then I'm all right, I thought. Tomorrow I'll go home. After I've slept. On the bedside table my watch said that it was eight o'clock. Eight p.m. I sighed deeply before sinking, irresistibly, into a deep, tranquil sleep.

I did not dream, or did not afterwards recall any dreams.

I am moving through corridors, I can see the ceilings, I am strapped onto some sort of vehicle.

It stops. Something is placed over my nose and mouth.

"You'll sleep now," says an oddly familiar voice.

I woke up at seven o'clock. There was a nurse beside my bed. She had been saying something to me, I guess to rouse me from my torpid state.

"Are they going to operate?" I asked.

"They have operated," said the nurse. "It's evening now. You've slept all day."

"But the pain stopped. It stopped last night."

"That's because your appendix had burst," she said. I was already sinking into sleep again. . . .

"Your appendix had already burst," she explained again. "All they took out was a tiny remnant. So we still have to disinfect you. You have peritonitis."

This was to justify an extremely painful injection just at the top of the right buttock. The pain had shot sharply down my leg. A searing pain.

"The poisons had already dispersed throughout your system, you see," continued this blandly cheerful middle-aged woman, whose name was Betty Something, "so we have to attack them with antibiotics and collect them with the drains."

"You certainly attacked *me*," I observed.

There are now three black rubber tubes stuck into the right side of my stomach. There is also a large, long, fresh scar beside them. "Dr. Palmer is famous for his large incisions," Betty had volunteered. "It's his signature."

Dr. Palmer. Carl's father? It must have been. It was appropriate somehow. I had not saved Carl from the world's poisons, but now Carl's father had rescued me. Again. And thereby somehow *claimed* me, even if I never saw the man again. I had not wanted to see him again after our unavoidable conversation about Carl's death; still, we had met several times more so that he could talk about it. I don't know who or what could possibly comfort his wife; I believe she is still more or less in pieces. Seeing no one.

These wounds would mark me forever. A signature. A brand name. Produce of Dr. Palmer. Like meat. The long scar and, no doubt, three smaller scars where swords have pierced me. Will they bleed in future like stigmata? The three tubes are slowly draining the poison out of me.

"The appendix is on the right side," I said. "But my pain was on the left."

"That's where it registered."

It was all fascinating in a way.

They fed me painkillers as well as injecting antibiotics. Soon I was groggy again, groggy most of the time.

My body was in shock. It had poisoned itself, was still poisoned. It had been cut open when it was too late to stop the poison. So three more holes had been cut into my stomach, and tubes inserted. I could not stop thinking about this.

I could not keep down even mushy food. So they put me on intravenous feeding. Another tube was stuck with a needle into the top of my right hand — to keep me alive with nourishment.

I was inhibited about farting. I could not piss at all. My body was too shocked, too violated, it seems. So I had to be catheterized. Yet another tube was inserted, this time into my penis. I felt violated utterly now. It didn't even work very well. The orderly who performed the task was openly disgusted by it.

Carl's father came to speak to me on the third day after the operation. I was woozy but I heard him.

"You've got to make more effort. Even if you just change your position in the bed more frequently. You've got to help your body start working again.

"You don't even move, they tell me. It's as if you didn't want to help yourself."

Like Carl. Who *could* not help himself.

"You can survive, you know," said Dr. Palmer.

The yellow-cream walls oppressed me. They were subtly reminiscent of vomit. They changed their color with the changing light. I wanted to shut them out, sleep forever. To shut out this whole hospital that was noisy both night and day with people, talk, cries, blaring radios.

My roommate was a middle-aged Italian, a heart patient named Convertini. He was recovering from a "minor" attack. Each afternoon he was visited by three or four women dressed in black who babbled on vivaciously and at length in Italian. I would fall in and out of my trance hearing them.

When I was more or less awake and we were alone,

Convertini would speak to me cheerfully. In broken English. He seemed to be a good man.

Then I would return to my own world.

It is the wood behind the beach. The clearing. Lisan takes my hand and leads me there.

"You killed me," she says quietly, "but I forgive you. Only now you have to join me here."

"I want to," I say to her.

The forest, which has sometimes seemed empty, is in fact highly populated. There are peaceful, benign Indians wearing their colorful robes. There are hearty, smiling explorers from France and England: gentlemen adventurers. It's like a wax museum come alive. It's wonderful to watch: an endless spectacle. History persisting.

There are also, every afternoon, many fat, happy, gesticulating Italian women dressed in black.

Lisan and I walk, hand in hand, for what seems like hours. We don't speak much. The forest is apparently endless. Always in the background is the faint roaring of the falls.

Once, briefly, I glimpse Carl in the center of a group of laughing young people. They seem to be picnicking. He waves at us in a friendly way. We wave back as we go by.

Whole days pass this way. In this magic kingdom.

One day Lester takes us to see the wise old man of the woods. He is an Italian, Lester says, and very wise. We find him seated on a large tree stump. He is a kind of dwarf with a thick white mustache, large, eloquent brown eyes, and long wiry white hair. He looks to me rather like photographs of Albert Einstein, but of course Einstein is not Italian. He can read minds, I discover.

"I am Dr. Enrico Fermi. Instead," he adds in a kindly way. He has only a slight accent, unlike Convertini.

"I have helped to make the bomb, you understand. Because it is time to clean out that world. We must finish with it and start over."

Somehow I have come to the forest's edge. I have come out of the woods. I am alone.

I am standing at the edge of the cliff, at the edge of the waterfall.

I think: it must be time now. So let it happen. "The waters are calling me." I can hear Lisan's voice in the call of the waters. Where is she? Among so many voices.

The waters are green and blue and white, dazzling white, as they stretch themselves luxuriantly, seductively, over the rock of the cliff. The rack and the rock, I think.

Then I look up from the falls and over the river to the American side. In the sky are four bright lights approaching rapidly. Each is pulsing, with brilliant red and blue and yellow lights alternating. Flying saucers, I think. But they are round or oblong, not like saucers at all.

Then the first bomb falls. A blinding flash. White, utter white — a white sky.

An apartment building across the river is disintegrating before my eyes. The walls blacken, then burst, and inside all is flame. I see another explosion further off. Then another. Another. The city is in flames before my open eyes. Odd that I'm not blind, that I'm not blinded, I think.

But I can feel myself rising now, slowly rising, off the ground, out of bed, rising, rising over the holocaust that has finally come, till I can look down on it, down on the burning city and the pounding falls, down on the bed and the room with the other bed and the man in it and the women in black still babbling, birdlike, in a foreign tongue.

Explosions are setting off new explosions now, there is a chain reaction. People are running into the streets in panic, only to die in the spreading, unstoppable fires. The furious fire-storm. A wind of flame. Cars, trees, whole streets are ablaze.

Now I am only in the room, I am hovering just below the ceiling as a slim, naked youth, myself, struggles out of bed beneath me, while the others, the several black-clad women and the man in the other bed, turn to look at him in sudden alarm.

"Ring for an orderly," says Convertini. The i.v. has come unstuck from the youth's hand, I see. But I am detached from this, from everything, I am separate now from all those tubes. No ties, no strings, I think. I am going to continue to rise above this, above the spreading explosions, above the death of the world, the anguished dying planet.

Lisan comes out of the woods into the light. She is wearing a long white dress that reflects the atomic sunlight, dazzling my eyes. She is beckoning. She is the messenger sent for me.

I begin to climb the sandy hill toward her. She stands by an opening, a kind of natural gateway into the green forest. There is birdsong, music. A world of colors, light and dark commingled. She will lead me. She will lead me now to the sun-dappled clearing where I belong, where we have both always belonged.

FIFTEEN

◆

(*The stage represents a dim forest. Human shapes in a small glade are gradually discernible, though shadowy. Each is isolated, singular. There is an Indian, splendid in ornamental robes, also an explorer, a trader, a Jesuit missionary, a huckster, a pair of honeymooners facing in different directions, and a half-undressed, beautiful blonde movie star with one milky breast exposed to view, spotlit. In the center of the stage is Angelo. He is completely naked, apelike, powerful. His costume is his body. Lisan is not to be seen. Angelo alone speaks. He speaks deliberately, slowly, in a low, growling voice. The other figures remain motionless around him, statue-like: a tableau of waxworks.*)

ANGELO:

Good evening, ladies and gentlemen.
   I am Hinun.
   Yes, that's right. I'm the god of this place.
   That's because I understand power.
   Therefore I have *become* Hinun. Or, rather, he has become me.

The process is called historical necessity. Historical inevitability.

If the waters fall, the chemicals will flow. My father made his money in chemicals. After the war he advised the military about the feasibility of chemical warfare. It was, he said, the wave of the future. The bomb was, he said, too wasteful of property. He was quite serious.

When we were small he took us to see the falls. This was, he said, one of the seven wonders of the modern world. (He was rather vague about the other six.)

For him capitalism meant selling the public, including the military, what it wanted. And, of course, what you can persuade it to want.

So that's what I did too. It's just the same. There was, is (believe it or not) a growing public demand for heroin. For speed. For cocaine. The latest thing is "crack" — cocaine plus baking soda baked into rock form. It gives, in a few seconds, a terrific five-minute high followed by deep depression, a real downer. You want more right away. It's the perfect product — highly addictive very fast. At this moment in history fourteen-year-olds are selling it on the streets in California. Or selling their bodies for it. And their masters are just now cracking the Canadian market too — you'll pardon my bad pun. It's a weakness I have. Puns I mean.

Yes. After the war I saw my chance and took it. I was only following in my father's highly profitable footsteps.

How he always hated me. So I wanted to outdo him. I wanted everything that was his. And to possess it more fully than he could bring himself to do. For he did love her.

As Hinun demanded the sacrifice of the maiden. So did I. I separated her from them. Forever.

I killed too. Sometimes. Deliberately, consciously —

not like him. More like a conscious god. Till they got me. Cut my thick throat. Too bad.

But that's the world. I had my day. My kicks. My method was to beat it up and then fuck it. Literally. I made each of my "*associates*", my subordinates, submit to me. At least once. It was the rite of passage. If they wanted to be cut in, they lay down for it, white or black ass bared. I developed a real taste for this. It's total power over someone's being. To violate and humiliate him.

You think I'm a monster?

(Pause)

Of course I am. It's my role in life, in the universe. I'm a god. Gods are wholly arbitrary, cruel or kind on whim. Animal. Sometimes not even conscious. Forces of nature. *Aren't they?*

That's the world.

I was ugly, so the world punished me. They laughed at me at school because I was so clumsy. Not coordinated. Not good at sports. Wholly without grace. Outsized, grotesque. I was Quasimodo, Caliban. My own society mother disliked me and avoided me. Voided me. My father hated me and beat me. Only my pretty little sister loved me. The princess and the court monster.

So I broke her. I broke her into pieces. She was as beautiful as I was ugly, so I loved her and I hated her. I separated her from them. From their hypocrisy.

I had no illusions about the world. Business is business.

I had nightmares. I had horrible nightmares sometimes if I slept alone. That's why I wanted Larry. He *enjoyed* it. Someone always there to work it out on. If I woke up howling.

I might just howl now.

Or rather, I might roar. Like a god in agony.

Because it might be agony as much as anger. (It might also be impossible longing.)

Like a god's. A god's hoarse whispering. A god with his throat cut from ear to ear.

(He is silent now for a moment. Then he begins to make a hoarse, whispering sound. This grows and grows gradually in volume till it resembles an old-fashioned train whistle. A train whistle that speaks from the distance of escape to other places, even other times. Then it seems part growl and part howl. It is a long-drawn-out cry of pain such as Olivier or Gielgud at the height of their powers might have brought off as Lear or Oedipus. It is louder and louder till, suddenly

it ceases. Abruptly. At the same instant the stage is plunged into total darkness.

In the background, faintly, can be heard the steady, reassuring roaring of the falls.)

SIXTEEN

◆

I am so calm now. The crisis is past. I will live. I am recovering now. But I am not the same.

Before antibiotics I would certainly have died. I would have had my wish.

Convertini had left and had been replaced by a whining local bureaucrat with a hernia. This man was inordinately proud of being head of the local P.U.C. He was also very demanding. He pestered the nurses constantly about trivialities. He complained of pain frequently. Ron rather despised him for being such a crybaby. But at least, he reflected, Mr. P.U.C. would not slip away quietly, as he himself might well have done; his whining at least made him a social being (as Dr. Johnson had once observed, speaking of the value of complaint). Ron knew quite well the reprehensibility of his own stoic solipsism. But he was too weak, too tired to show much sympathy to the man.

He did not dream now.

This is the afterlife, he told himself. It's very calm in the afterlife. One does not dream.

He took a detached interest in his drains and dressings now. Even the stink was interesting. He observed his body as it gathered the strength to heal itself.

Friends came. Mike came. His mother came. But he was not yet able to respond very much to anyone. He was quietly polite but he wished they would go away. He even offered, somewhat mischievously, to remove one of his dressings and show Steve the wound where one of the drains had been removed. He was secretly amused by the look of apprehension that came over Steve's face then. He soon left. Nobody else wanted to dwell on the details. But he found them interesting now.

On the shelf against the cream wall were two bottles of detergent, used to wash Ron and the P.U.C. man without removing them from their beds. His eye often fell on them. One, he decided, was male, the other female. Their shapes were formed by loose clerical robes. A bishop and an abbess. It was like the fantasies of his childhood, the characters he had found in the bedroom's abstract wallpaper.

He could eat normally now. And shit in the bathroom by himself. He took the antibiotics orally and painlessly now.

The tubes, one by one, were removed, but the dressings remained, and were changed regularly. The wounds continued to drain. Till, in the third week, two of them stopped. But the third continued.

He could get up and move around now. Though there was nowhere to go.

One day they removed the stitches from his wounds. Only the four scars, which ached a little for months, years, afterwards, remained.

He was weak. Though he was slim to begin with, he had lost at least twenty pounds and could scarcely recognize himself in the mirror. He was someone else now.

Perhaps that's why she changed her mind and sent me back. So that I could become someone else. Start anew. It was an act of generosity, at the last.

After three weeks they decided to release him. He dressed in clothes that hung on him oddly. His mother and her husband came to pick him up.

One dressing remained, and he had to change it himself, since the wound was still draining slightly.

He stayed home for a week. Then he went back to work, still weak, against his family's objections. He needed all the money he could get to go to Europe.

One day, when he was changing his dressing, he noticed a tiny dark spot in the oozing swamp of his wound. He pinched at it with his fingernails then pulled, and to his surprise drew out a long black thread. It was a bit of stitch that had not been removed but had remained to irritate the wound. Which healed quickly thereafter.

He was pleased in a peculiar way to have performed the last act of surgery himself.

Now I was cut off from the past. Detached from it. Calm. Free. But not without reminders, conditions.

I began to see my little brush with death as unimportant. I had almost been a victim but survived. The real victims were my father, Carl, Lisan, even Larry. And yes. Even Angelo. They were all victims of our tainted North American history. That poisoning of the once good earth. Even my own petty story could be seen as part of that large general tragedy.

A paranoid vision? Perhaps. But it was all I had. Elsewhere, of course, people lived on, I mean, *good* people still lived good and useful lives. I knew that but could not concentrate on it.

And then there came, that summer, yet another death.

Not, ironically, mine, which had seemed imminent. A more significant and symbolic death. The death of the goddess. Another warning there. This one distant but inescapable — because notorious, world famous.

For a day or two that summer the newspapers were full of it. The death of the unofficial goddess of love. For Marilyn had, apparently, taken her own life. Although we know such overdoses — for one addicted to barbiturates — can be accidental. So perhaps it was. But Marilyn was a focus of large forces, lover of powerful, compromised men. In later years came theories that she might even have been murdered.

Her life has been seen as exemplary. She is, for many, the tragic saint or martyred whore. A beautiful creation thrown up, served up (as on a half-shell), by America, and then destroyed by America.

For years she had drifted from man to man, Hollywood to New York and back again, from great success to personal anxiety and crisis, from performers to intellectuals to politicians, from aching childlessness to addiction to apparent suicide. Abused in childhood, she could not cope with adult life or identity, despite being adored by millions. She had sought out love as power, and power abused her. She had sung "Happy Birthday" in a public tribute to President John Kennedy when he turned forty-five. She was the preeminent victim of the times.

I felt as if I knew her.

I remembered that day, some ten years before, by the Rainbow Bridge. How she walked across the street to the hotel. How I rode my bicycle close up beside her. How I almost touched her.

As an actress she proved herself, in time, a gifted light comedienne. Not at all the avatar, perched atop the falls, of all that torrent of pagan passion. Too messed up personally, really, to have that kind of unbridled passion or power to spare. But the myth would persist, of course. And thus had its own truth.

Dead at thirty-six. For how could she have lived to be old?

Then I remembered Mary-Jane. Who had wanted to be Marilyn. Did she still? Where was she? She would grieve, wherever she was.

As for me, I was moved but still calm. For I had gone away myself but had returned again.

So calm. He was so calm now. Each August day he returned from work and sat in his room looking out the window. It framed a tapestry of leaves and trees growing up the side of the escarpment. Squirrels and chipmunks gamboled there. Small birds perched and sang in the branches over the flagstone terrace laid by Mr. Hendricks. Thyme and Queen Anne's lace grew between the stones. Ron thought of the framed scene as somehow medieval. Elizabethan or late medieval in feeling, like "Greensleeves". Timeless and yet placed in time.

Somewhere, in the imagination perhaps, everything that had happened was still happening. The green world both persists and dies, he thought, endlessly. . . .

Each evening as dusk fell — and it fell a little earlier now each evening — he watched the tapestry fade out. Like a film dissolving. He never wanted to do anything else.

I'm living in a private world, he mused. The world through the window. Like . . . like my grandfather, he realized in mild shock.

I seem to have *become* my grandfather.

After Labor Day I left the bridge and got some odd, temporary jobs — in supermarkets and bowling alleys — for a couple of weeks. Then I was hired as seasonal labor at a winery which was, conveniently, about a mile away from my mother's house. I could walk to and from work.

Here I joined several young men in their late twenties — uneducated and working only seasonally — in a shed which received the husks of grapes from the floor above. These were repeatedly lifted on a sort of blanket and thrown off one end of the shed onto the ground, from which local farmers collected them to use as fertilizer. The husks stank, and after a while so did the men. It was an exceedingly boring job, and especially tiring for someone in a weakened state who was not accustomed to physical labor. But I forced myself. I didn't want to seem weak. And I didn't tell my coworkers that I was a university graduate. I was so thin then that they thought I was a teenager. They assumed I had nothing much to contribute to their man's talk of drinking and screwing around on their wives. These were their only subjects. To them I looked like a kid. I was in fact twenty-four.

But they were right in a way. I had never lived in their world, and did not pretend to know about it. I listened to their crude jokes and stories with apparent appreciation and thus got along all right. I did not dream of telling them my own story. I was in disguise now, at least among the living.

When they were bored these men would, one or two of them at a time, sneak up to the upper floor and drink unprocessed wine from the taps on the rubber hoses that ran between the wine vats. I was not much tempted — I thought I had had enough of rubber tubes. Inevitably one of the men would go too far and become drunk and obstreperous. He was then sent home by the boss, but always taken back again. These outbursts were expected, part of the ordinary life of the winery in the busy season. It was all interesting in its way. A slice of ordinary life.

I stayed all through October. At some point, no doubt because I was physically slight and made little difference there, I was moved from the husk shed to the floor upstairs and given the task of stirring the large vats of wine. They can be sure I won't be drinking this swill, I thought. I would stand on a ladder and stir the wine in the vat with a long pole. When it shone directly through the open door-way on one wall of the large room — in fact, there was no door, though this was the second or third story — the setting sun made gorgeous rainbows in the wine and in the fumes rising from the wine. I wondered at times if the fumes were affecting me. These rainbows were more pungent than the rainbows of the falls.

On one shift I worked afternoon and evening. After which I walked home along the old country road to the fashionable new subdivision on the edge of the escarpment, my tall rubber boots stinking of raw wine and attracting clouds of fruit flies. I was a walking cloud, a plague. I was a corrupt, physical creature like the rest of them now. I was always tired and always strangely happy. When I arrived I had to leave my boots outside the front door, since Harriet would not allow them in her dream house. The flies lingered overnight.

Nothing can disturb this calm. Not even the worst thing.

You see, he explains silently, it didn't really happen. It's not due yet. Or I'd be dead.

Seven p.m. on a Monday. October 22, 1962. The voice of power.

"The purpose of these bases can be none other than to provide a nuclear strike capability against the western hemisphere. . . ."

The voice is calm, grave, deliberate. It has the peculiar Boston accent and intonation that have become familiar. The famous youthful face is here too, with the shock of hair on top. It is composed of black and white dots, dots projected. The face is *composed*, in both senses. This is all unreal.

". . . intermediate range ballistic missiles . . . capable of striking most of the major cities in the western hemisphere, ranging as far north as Hudson Bay, Canada, and as far south as Lima, Peru. . . ."

The three silhouettes are silent in the white television glare. From outside they appear to be shadows in a pale-blue light. Ghosts. Ron is outside in the yard now, looking in on the three still figures. One of whom is himself.

". . . an explicit threat to the peace and security of all the Americas. . . ."

Has it come at last? After the great preliminary wars, after the long preparation? After the eerie twilight of the fifties? The unreal calm? Someone near him is thinking these thoughts.

". . . this secret, swift, extraordinary buildup of communist missiles . . . this sudden, clandestine decision . . . is a deliberately provocative and unjustified change in the status quo which cannot be accepted by this country. . . ."

The status quo. What can the man mean? Who speaks so calmly of "unmistakable evidence", the removal of strategic nuclear weapons, of war in which "even victory" would be "ashes in our mouth". It is all words. Words.

". . . now further action is required, and it is under way, and these actions may only be the beginning. . . ."

Nuclear war. The man is speaking calmly of nuclear war.

" . . . neither will we shrink from that risk at any time it must be faced. . . ."

Still, they were silent, they made no protest. The face on the television screen spoke on. Of the "quarantine" of ships, of continued "close surveillance of Cuba and its military buildup", of "further action", and of "any eventualities". The armed forces of America are on alert.

The speech is over. Though there are shocked (or perhaps elated?) news commentators talking away excitedly now, they do not really hear them. Now they are able to speak for themselves.

"You can't go now. There could be a war," she said.

"I'm going," said Ron.

"We live in dangerous times," observed Mr. Hendricks. He was trying to be steady, but Ron could see that he was shaken too. He forgot for a moment that the man had been in the last war. He felt a cool, and a cruel, satisfaction and superiority.

The falls will be a prime target, he thinks. The hydro power will have to be destroyed.

"The Russians will back down," Ron announces confidently. "It will all blow over." He did not know if he really believed this. The truth was that in some strange way he no longer cared.

"I think that too," says Mr. Hendricks. "If we believe they are rational. But we can't ever be sure."

"I'm going," Ron says once again.

Within a week the Russians did back down. Ron found himself humming Tom Lehrer's ditty, "We'll all go together when we go." To Harriet's obvious irritation.

He was now planning to travel cheaply to Scotland on a freighter that was to leave Montreal some time later in November.

"I want to see the world while it's still there," he wise-cracked. His mother and Mr. Hendricks thought his jokes were in poor taste.

Privately, he was not so cocky as he seemed. He kept remembering something Steve had said. The only remark of Steve's that had ever stayed in his mind.

It was in August when Steve and his family had come out for dinner. Afterwards they all sat out on the terrace looking for satellites in the sky.

Eventually everyone except Steve and Ron went in.

"Remember," Steve said, "how Carl thought he saw a U.F.O. in California. Poor Carl. I guess he went off the deep end there."

"U.F.O.s," pronounced Ron, "are the cargo cult of North America. Everybody wants some Big Daddy from the sky to rescue us from war and pollution. What we've made of the world."

"Maybe," Steve said.

Then he said: "How do you feel, really?"

"With my hands," said Ron flippantly.

"Oh come on. You know what I mean. You must have been pretty shaken about being so sick."

"It was just something that happened. I'm okay, now."

"Oh come on."

"It wasn't so bad," said Ron. He was so calm.

"Well . . ." said Steve, who seemed troubled. "Maybe you see it that way now. But you were pretty far gone, I'm told. My grandmother even had a saying for it. She'd say: I guess you felt the brush of the angel's wing."

It was so dark now that he could not see Steve's face very well. He was never afterwards to be certain just what expression had accompanied his friend's uncharacteristically poetic words.

EPILOGUE: The Wound

. . . the rainbows over the Falls were like the arts and beauty and goodness, with regard to the stream of life — caused by it, thrown upon its spray, but unable to stay or direct or affect it, and ceasing when it ceased. . . . The river, with its multitudinous waves and its single current, likens itself to a life, whether of an individual or a community . . . both men and nations are hurried onwards to their ruin or ending as inevitably as this dark flood. . . . And as incessant, as inevitable, and as unavailing as the spray that hangs over the Falls, is the white cloud of human crying.
— Rupert Brooke, *Letters From America*

The story I have told you is perhaps true, perhaps not. I do not, cannot, finally know. For I have long ago been diagnosed as a controlled, or "borderline", schizophrenic, reasonably stable and responsible so long as I take my medication, but perhaps not always quite in touch with objective reality — indeed, not always convinced there is any such thing. So perhaps those of you who live in a more stable world should not entirely trust me. After all, I am now a novelist (i.e., a professional liar) as well. For I have here told my "borderline" story in the form of a novel.

Here is the rest of that story.

While I was tossing about on a freighter in the stormy north Atlantic, my long lost and only recently recovered grandfather died. I learned this only when, weeks later, I collected some mail at Canada House in London. It was another death — a peaceful one. A closed chapter. As my new life began.

From December of 1962 till August of 1963 I traveled here and there about Europe, part of the time with a girl from Toronto whom I later married. But we were only friends then, companions. In Europe I was a young tourist, like thousands of others.

I had survived, as Dr. Palmer said I could. He himself died five years later in a traffic accident — he was drunk, his wife had recently committed suicide. With pills. But I survived to meet my own later life's disasters. As most of us do.

Meanwhile I recovered my physical strength, even while traveling. I tried to heal myself. And in my mind I said farewell to my lost love Lisan. And to my doomed childhood friend Carl as well. May they forgive me as I forgive them. And Larry too, wherever he is.

In Rome, similarly, I made a ritual farewell to my mother. I came upon her not quite by chance inside St. Peter's, where she looked out at me from within Michelangelo's celebrated Pietà. I had expected, of course, to be impressed by this very famous work, but I was not prepared to be so deeply moved as I was — after all, I am not a Catholic and have not acquired any great sympathy for the Church or its rituals. But Michelangelo's art goes beyond

Catholicism, even beyond Christianity. For here sits the eternal Mother holding her broken, or mortally wounded, Son. She is larger than life-size. She is larger than he is, she seems almost to surround him like the triangle of his destiny, as if he has been at last returned to the womb of Eternity from whence he came. She is more like the great goddess meting out life and death than the Virgin of tradition. She is Eternity in love with the productions of time.

I thought as well then of the young girl visited by the angel. For I too had looked on the angel in my youth. As had Lisan.

That spring I moved in a kind of dream. On Crete I lived in a cave for some weeks like a monk in the desert. Like a new soul in its cocoon. Each morning I would swim naked in the sea. I was calm in a way that I cannot recapture now.

I then spent the later spring and summer in London. I saw my friend Sandra again.

When my money ran out that August, I got a cheap student boat from Amsterdam to New York. Once *New* Amsterdam. It was overcrowded — about six of us to a cabin — mainly with horny young Americans. The boy in the bunk below me, for instance, was particularly successful in persuading a succession of little girls into his narrow bed under cover of darkness. Each night the rest of us, if awake, could hear the beast with two backs going at it none too quietly. In fact, the whole ship was a throbbing dynamo of young sexual activity despite the almost complete lack of privacy. But I was detached from all of this, I felt infinitely older than these students. I was still St. Ronald of the caves. They might be the shock troops of the oncoming sexual revolution, but I felt temporarily retired.

Meanwhile the world continued. Marilyn Monroe might be dead, but President Kennedy, whom some said

had been her lover, was still alive and vigorous. Khru-
shchev still represented the Soviet Union, and they had
reached an understanding. A nuclear-test-ban treaty had
been signed. The president called it a small candle in the
darkness. "So shines a good deed in a naughty world."
Perhaps there would be peace after all. Perhaps the world,
after the turmoil of all the war years before, had at last
become as calm as I was.

New York. Because I had never been there before, I was
still voyaging. Even the Statue of Liberty was an "event"
— like the leaning tower of Pisa, upon which I had
stumbled one evening by accident. Miss Liberty wel-
comed me back to America. "Land of the free." I was like
an immigrant from Europe, or perhaps from death. I stayed
at the YMCA for several days. I went to see *Who's Afraid of
Virginia Woolf?* on the stage and to the somewhat ridiculous
film *Cleopatra*. I couldn't afford to do very much or stay
very long.

And so I headed north to my real home. Canada, land of
the unfree. My mother and Steve's father still lived, of
course, in the subdivision on the escarpment. I did not
belong there as I had in the house in town. But it was a
pleasant place to visit. On a clear day you could see from
the picture window all the way across the lake to Toronto.
City of my future.

My mother seemed happy enough. So did Mr. Hendricks. They were thinking of wintering in Florida.

I saw Steve and his family, of course. We were now
relatives of a sort. I saw my unchanged brother and his
family too. Good enough people — but already part of my
past.

One evening I drove into town in Mr. Hendricks' car to
look at the old house. I discovered that the new owners,
who were immigrant Dutch rather than merely Dutch in

ancestry like my stepfather, had replaced the grass of the
front lawn with gravel. More practical, I suppose they
thought. But they had left the lilac tree intact, and I was
grateful for that.

My father and I had sat on that porch. My mother and I
had talked in the room inside. I had taken Lisan upstairs.
Once.

I hadn't planned to do more than look briefly — I
thought I might then go to a movie — but Mrs. Wensing
spotted me standing out there on the street. We had met a
few years before when she worked for a while at Table
Rock House. So she came out to speak to me. It was just
after sundown.

She insisted on giving me a tour of the house. They had
tidied it up a great deal. It made me think of Lisan's return
to her parents' former house in Buffalo. But this one had
always been more modest. And this return was much less
traumatic. I was glad the house was in good Dutch hands,
just as I was glad my mother was in good hands. So I
congratulated Mrs. Wensing on all her "improvements".
She was obviously proud of what she had accomplished in
a fairly short time. The house had needed many repairs.

She insisted on making some coffee. We sat in the
living–room by the window as it grew dusky both outside
and in. I gave her my recent impressions of Amsterdam
while I wondered how soon I could go without offending
her. Her husband was working nights, and her teenage
children were off somewhere too. She seemed glad of company.

There was someone, a man or a boy, outside in the
darkening yard, outlined against the dim white gravel. He
was standing beyond the porch by the lilac tree looking
directly toward the window beside which we sat. He wore
cheap pants, a plain shirt much like my own. He had very

strange, large eyes which stood out boldly, though his other features were indistinct in the gathering dusk. Looking at him there and beginning to feel slightly alarmed at the intensity of his eyes (were they menacing? accusing?), I was suddenly conscious as well of the faint but distinct roaring of the falls in the background. It had been there all along, and subliminally felt.

I turned back to Mrs. Wensing. She too had looked out the window, following my gaze. But I realized then that she did not see anyone. At least, she saw no one unexpected or alarming. She went on talking about old Amsterdam. Her lost home. As this was mine.

After a while I saw that the man was gone. I didn't see him move away. He was simply gone.

I thought immediately afterwards that it must have been one of Mrs. Wensing's teenage sons who didn't want to encounter a strange visitor to the house. But I knew better even then.

And I had other thoughts that came unbidden. Both sinister and whimsical.

Driving home in the darkness I thought perhaps he was a traveler from the night side, a messenger, a "connection". An alien from some other space. The "land of faery" perhaps. The invisible. He was a "spaceman", perhaps, from some other dying planet. A dark fallen angel. Or perhaps he was one of the "Neutrals" who still partly occupied this place. He had haunted eyes because of all the darkness he had seen, and he knew no rest. He was positively Byronic, I thought later, even a little ridiculous.

Whereas I myself was then so calm. So collected, in control. Anti-romantic.

Oh yes. I was all of that for a while. At that time.

It was, is, I think, a good time in which to lay to rest this particular story. For what followed of good and ill, strangely mingled, is not strictly part of it. But you may guess that the messenger returned. More than once.

I know now for certain who he was, who he is.

ABOUT THE AUTHOR

Tom Marshall was born in Niagara Falls, Ontario, in 1938 and attended public and high school there. He is now a full professor of English at Queen's University in Kingston, where he has taught since 1964. He has published eight books of poetry, three books of criticism, and a collection of short stories. This is his third published novel.